RETURN TO CHRISTMAS TOWN

RETURN TO CHRISTMAS TOWN

D.W. SAUR

POLAR PRESS LLC

Contents

35 Aftermath   191

Return To Christmas Town

By D.W. Saur

© Copyright 2023 D.W. Saur

Published By

www.polarpressbooks.com

In Memory of
Kevin and Chris

Author's Note

I want to thank everyone for their support over the past few years. Not only would this journey not have continued, but *The Return to Christmas Town* would have never started. Many reached out after reading *The Last Christmas* asking if there would be a sequel. At the time I said no because I loved the story and didn't think it needed a follow-up.

I'm not certain about the timeline, but at some point, my brain wouldn't let it go and a story began to unfold. I started typing away, and before long, *Return To Christmas Town* was born. I loved revisiting Christmas Town, and though this is a sequel, it can be read as a standalone. However, before continuing to the next page, one may want to consider reading *The Last Christmas* to become familiar with Christmas Town and those who reside within the pages.

Lastly, I want to end this brief note as it began.

Thank you for your continued support. I'm forever grateful you've joined me for another work and hope you enjoy *Return To Christmas Town.*

I

Family Meeting: Part I

The hustle and bustle of the diner was drowned out by the ringing of the phone. The vibration was like a freight train barreling down the tracks, rattling the silverware and plate. T.J. looked down at the name and then at the headline on the paper. The white letters of Aunt Beth acted like the bat signal.

T.J. sat his fork down, picked up the phone, took a deep breath, and answered, "Good morning, Aunt Beth."

"Get here now," Beth demanded.

T.J. looked down at his unfinished breakfast. "I'm in the middle of eating."

"I don't care. Get here now," she ordered.

"Let me guess, this is about the paper."

"Of course, it's about the paper. Your uncle and I have been pacing around the office waiting for you to get here so we can talk about it."

"So talk. Put me on speaker."

"He's stubborn like you and Mom." She paused, then said, "You're on speaker."

"Morning, Uncle Jon."

"Morning, T.J. You're going to have to forgive your aunt. She's just worried."

"As she should be," T.J. said.

T.J. heard his aunt's voice shriek through the phone. He could picture her pacing, hands on her hips. Nonetheless, he made out: "Hang up the phone, Jonathan. He's not going to help."

"Calm down, Beth, and T.J. dial it back a bit."

"Sorry, but I know this is serious. I'm just as worried as you are."

"Are you?" Beth asked. "Because the moment you read a resort was being built across the street you should've been here."

"What do you want me to do? If I were there, then I'd be watching you pace around while shouting god knows what." T.J. bounced his head from side to side. "Much like you are now, so pretend I'm there."

"I'm not shouting," Beth insisted in a calmer yet still high-pitched tone.

T.J. dug his fork under his eggs and informed, "I'm working on a couple of things that may slow down the build."

"Wait. Did you know about this before today?" Jonathan asked.

"I did, but I couldn't say anything." He quickly shoved the eggs in his mouth and chewed as fast as he could.

"Why would you keep something like this to yourself?" Beth yelled. T.J. said nothing as he continued to chew.

"T.J.? Are you there?" Jonathan asked.

T.J. swallowed and answered, "I'm here. I told you I was eating, and I think Beth's reaction has answered her question. Look, there's no reason to panic just yet. Let's see if my plan works."

"What do you have in mind?" Jonathan asked.

"I'll fill you in soon, but first I'm going to get back to my breakfast. I'll be over this afternoon."

T.J. hung up the phone and focused back on his meal.

2

Do You Mind?

"Excuse me, but do you mind if I sit with you?" T.J. looked up from his paper and leaned to his right. He gazed past the stranger to see that all the stools, tables, and booths were full, and he turned around to see the same. "I'm sorry. It's the only seat left."

"Have a seat." T.J. put down his paper and waved at the empty chair.

"Thank you." The woman pulled out the chair and took a seat. "I'm—"

"Sydney. Sydney Garcia."

"Have we met?" T.J. turned over the paper and tapped at the headline, *Garcia Entertainment Purchases 400 Acres. Looks to Buy 800 More.* Sydney started to grab her things. "I'm just going to get my order to go."

"Relax. I'm T.J., and there's no judgment, contempt, or whatever at this table."

She tilted her head slightly and squinted. Rubbing her forehead, she asked, "Why?"

"Why what?"

"Why would you let me sit with you when you know why I'm here?" The waitress plopped a to-go cup on the table and filled it with coffee. Once full, Sydney said, "Thank you."

"I'll be back in a few to take your order," the waitress informed.

Sydney watched her walk off and leaned toward T.J. "See. That. That right there. I've been met with nothing but hostility since I got here. We chose this area because it's a friendly, quaint, and small town."

"I guess that was your first mistake."

"Tell me about it." Sydney leaned back in her chair. "There were plenty of places to pick, but I just had to pick the one with the worst attitude."

"The location and the people are fine—the way you picked is the issue." T.J. leaned forward. Sydney quickly leaned back in to hear what he was going to say. Less than a ruler separated the two. "We aren't a poll."

"Oh." Sydney leaned back. "So we've offended you."

"Yes, and more."

Sydney bit her lip and nodded. She raised her hand and asked, "What do you mean more?"

"The plan for your business is going hurt this county."

"Hurt it? We're building in the next county over. I'm only here because this place has the closest motel to the property."

"Yes, but the loss of jobs—"

"Loss of jobs?" T.J. nodded. "I can hire at least eight hundred people right now."

"Sure, you can hire them now, but first you're going to cause them to lose their job."

"See, that's why I'm here. We aren't planning on putting people out of business."

"I'm sure that's what you're telling people, but think about it." T.J. didn't say anything and just stared at Sydney. Her blank expression revealed her lack of understanding. "Christmas Town is a staple of this community. All you plan to do will siphon business, which will cause a thriving business to go on life support until it's forced to close shop."

"That's not our intent, and if they can't compete, then I'm sorry but that's business." T.J. pointed to an area behind Sydney. She turned to look. "What am I looking at?"

"See the table with the four ladies? One of them is in a wheelchair."

"Yes." Sydney turned back to T.J.

"Ms. Thomas was in a bad wreck a few years back where her husband was killed and she was paralyzed. Her husband was one of the most caring souls I've ever met. Both would give you the shirt off their back if you were in need."

"Let me guess, she's employed by Christmas Town."

"She is. She became the manager of their cabins, but the four ladies there make the best winter hats. Every morning they come here to have breakfast, head to their office at Christmas Town, and make hats while ensuring the cabins are ready for guests.

The hats are sold by Christmas Town and are one of their bestsellers."

"It's a heart-warming story. The good news is that if Christmas Town were to fold, then we could use someone with her experience."

"That's the difference. You want to use them while this town wants to provide for them. You see, Ms. Thomas became depressed and withdrew from everything. She was close to losing everything she had left until those three ladies stepped in. A lot happened, but the short version is that they started making hats that led to commission sales at Christmas Town and then managers of the cabins."

"You're wasting your breath T.J.," the waitress said. She glared at Sydney with a look that could only be defined as a death stare. "They don't care about small towns."

"Now, Melissa, you know that's not my way," T.J. said.

"I know." The smile Melissa gave T.J. faded as she looked at Sydney. "What can I get for you?"

Sydney looked at her watch. "Can I get two blueberry muffins and another coffee to go?"

Melissa replied, "Wouldn't have it any other way."

T.J. glanced back at Melissa. "Don't mind her. She's just protective of this place and its people."

Sydney nodded. "Seems like she's not the only one."

"I have stories like that for just about everyone in here."

"So Christmas Town is the savior of the community." Sydney raised her hands as if she were in church praising the almighty.

T.J. chuckled at her impersonation. "How long are you in town for?"

"Two weeks, maybe more. I have to—" Sydney stopped.

"Secure more land," T.J. finished for her.

Melissa returned with a bag, coffee, and a check. "Try not to ruin any more lives today."

"Not why I'm here," Sydney insisted. She reached into her purse and fumbled through it.

"I got this." T.J. grabbed the check and pulled a twenty and a ten out of his wallet. "Round up Melissa and the rest is for you."

"You got it." Melissa walked away without saying another word.

Still fumbling through her purse, Sydney said, "No, it's okay. I promise I can pay for my food."

"I know you can. I mean, it's not every day we get someone who walks in here whose company made over 300 million dollars for their records, twice as much from their movies, and even more than that from their stock investments."

Sydney stopped looking through her purse and returned her gaze to T.J. "Why do you know this? The article only said mega-million, which I still have issues with."

"I looked you up as soon as I heard your company was interested in land here."

"How did you find out?" Sydney stood up and stepped over to T.J.'s seat. "The sale only went public today."

T.J. got up and explained, "I have my ways. For example, I know you're going to see Mr. White once you leave here."

The red on her face signaled she was as mad as a kicked hornet's nest but her wide eyes showed intrigue. "How do you know that?"

"Your Mr. White's nine o'clock and I'm his ten." T.J. grabbed the paper from the table and started for the door.

Sydney caught up with him outside. "Why do you have a meeting with Mr. White?"

"Same reason as you."

"You can't go after that land," she informed. "We need—"

"Mr. White has just over four hundred acres that are adjacent to the property you just bought, which is also next to another two hundred acres. Mr. White is going to be a hard sell but Mr. Hall is ready to sign now. However, the properties are unique in shape and you want connecting properties, so you won't buy Hall's land without White's."

Sydney grabbed T.J. by the arm. She was gentle, but still, it was the gesture that caught T.J.'s attention. "Look, we don't know each other, but you need to understand that this deal is more than just about a company."

T.J. smiled. "Oh, I know what it's really about." Sydney looked baffled once more. "What are you driving?"

She shook her head and asked, "What? Why? The Tesla there." Sydney pointed to the red Tesla far to their right.

"I love electric cars as much as the next person but you can't take that to Mr. White's house."

"Let me guess, it shows I'm rich or out of touch."

"He knows you're rich, so you can cruise on in with a multi-million dollar sports car and he still wouldn't care. No, this is about the road. It has more holes than Swiss cheese; if you hit the right one, you'll be stuck. Come on." T.J. waved for Sydney to follow.

She followed him to his truck where he opened the door and

started to get in, but Sydney didn't follow. The truck started and T.J. was behind the wheel waving for her to join. She moved to the passenger side and motioned for him to roll down the window.

"You do understand that I know nothing about you and you're asking a woman to just hop in your car with you?"

"I do, but there are cameras, witnesses, and an itinerary that—"

"That will easily disappear and the people will say they have no idea what happened to me once I left the diner."

"Take a picture of me and my license plate. Send it to someone you trust and explain what you're doing so there's a record you can't erase."

Sydney immediately pulled out her phone and began taking pictures.

3

Friend or Foe

Sydney turned to T.J. and asked, "How old are you?"

"If it's considered rude to ask a woman that question, then why would you ask *me* that?"

"Because I think we are the same age or at least close to each other." T.J. took his eye off the road and looked at Sydney.

"If we are, then why is this relevant?"

"Don't give me that look."

"What look?"

"You know exactly what look. That squinty thing you're doing with your eyes. Like you're trying to figure out if I'm going to hit on you."

Turning back to the road, T.J. grinned. "I didn't think that at all. It's just an odd question."

"It's not odd. It's relevant."

"How so?"

"I'm twenty-five and know absolutely nothing about the people in my neighborhood and even less about the people who work for me. Assuming that you're my age, you not only know people's names but their stories. Oh, and you know the size and shape of their property." T.J. started to laugh and shook his head back and forth. "What's so funny?"

"My name isn't T.J.," he answered.

"But that's what the waitress said." T.J. turned to her and gave her a hard stare. "Melissa. That's what Melissa said."

"When I was a kid I absorbed everything. I could hear or see something and like magic, I knew it. I also did a lot of eavesdropping, which caused me to learn a lot of things I shouldn't have, but I did. When I heard something interesting I would go to the library and research it. We have an excellent town archive by the way.

"Well, one day there was an argument at the diner about some land. I went over to the three gentlemen and told them they were wrong. I picked up a kid's menu and crayons and drew their properties. The land in question was owned by the county and used as a draining pond, but it was so large that the farmers used it to water their crops. It was a hotter-than-usual summer with little rain, so the pond ran dry pretty quickly. Each of the farmers accused the other of stealing, but in a way, they were stealing from the county. I say, 'in a way' because the county would never press charges over using runoff water."

"So where does T.J. come into the picture?"

"They ran off to town hall to check the land records, came back, and proclaimed, 'We have a real T.J. Hooker on our hands.'"

"Who?"

"It was a show in early the '80s. T.J. was played by William Shatner, a former detective turned beat cop or something like that. I never watched it but you'll find a lot of Trekkies here who are obsessed with Shatner. Well, many of them are no longer with us, but since that day, I've been called T.J."

"That's an interesting story, but it leads to the question of the day."

"And that is?"

"What's your real name?"

T.J. turned to her and smiled a million-dollar smile. "Maybe you'll be here long enough to find out."

"Don't get your hopes up." Sydney turned to the window. "I know this is going to sound weird but do you have any advice for me for talking to Mr. White?"

"Isn't that something? Asking the competition for advice."

"I know you're not going to believe this but—"

"This is your shot, right?" T.J. looked over as Sydney turned her head. "Your dad considers this an easy deal but still wants to see if you can land it. If you secure this land, then you secure your stake in the company."

"The nickname of a detective suits you, but yes. This is my shot."

"First off, this is *a* shot, not your *only* shot. Your dad knows nothing about this area and you're going to find this will be far harder than you think. But—" T.J. held up a finger. "I'll give it to him that he knows the business."

"That he does, but you avoided the question. Do you have any advice?"

T.J. huffed. "Mr. White's family has owned that land

since before this was a county, and you have to understand that. You have to treat him like a person and not a business deal. When you see his land you have a vision of cabins or whatnot. When he looks at his land he sees his great-grandfather toiling away. He remembers building the deck on his house and the feel of driving the nail into the wood. This is a business deal to you, but for him, it's his life. His legacy."

"I never looked at it that way."

"Of course not and that's not your fault. No school teaches the human side of business and I don't mean an ethics course. I mean the human side. The side that helps you understand what it means to give up land that's been in your family for generations. Money can be a powerful lure for some, but for others, memories are the greater influence."

T.J. pulled off the main road and onto the dirt path that was Mr. White's driveway. They bounced left and right, up, and down. A car could've slowly navigated the holes and bumps but it would have been time-consuming and difficult. As the truck came to a halt next to an old wooden barn that had seen better days, T.J. leaned toward Sydney and waved at Mr. White sitting on the porch.

"Go on," T.J. urged.

"I must say, you've made me nervous."

When Sydney looked over, T.J. could tell she wasn't lying. She gripped her purse as though she was never going to let it go or perhaps swing it as hard as she could to eliminate the competition. T.J. placed a hand on her shoulder, she snapped her head over, and they locked eyes.

"Even if he doesn't pick you for the deal, I'll help you any way I can."

She took a deep breath and closed her eyes. "No, I got this. I have a great plan. You just have me rattled with your mind games. That's all."

And like a cloud releasing its rain, T.J. watched the weight of the world fall off her shoulders. She sat up straight, her hands loosened the grip on her purse, and she reached for the door.

"That's it." T.J. motioned for Sydney to shoo. "Get going."

He watched as she approached and introduced herself to Mr. White. The two went inside while he waited for her return. T.J. killed time by listening to the radio, and when Sydney returned, he took his leave. When they passed, it was nothing but a smile from Sydney. She sauntered toward the car as though she had sealed the deal and he was just wasting time. Ten minutes later, T.J. returned and started up the truck.

"What are you doing?" Sydney asked.

"Starting the truck. Then put it in reserve and take you to town."

"Ten minutes and you're done. I swear if you undercut me, I'll make you pay."

T.J. refused to get into a shouting match. "Look, there's no need for anger. Mr. White said he'll call us tomorrow with the decision." T.J. put the truck in reverse.

"Who are you?" Sydney demanded.

"Just a local boy with a trust fund and money to spend."

"I knew it!"

"What?"

"This whole 'I'm a good guy' routine. You're just like me.

A spoiled rich kid trying to make their mark. You don't want anyone to come here because you want it all yourself."

T.J. slammed on the brakes. Sydney jerked forward but was promptly pulled back by the seat belt. The fire Sydney lit in T.J. showed in his soul-piercing stare. The brown of his eyes might as well have been flames. His clenched jaw kept him from saying anything, but he didn't need to utter a word. Sydney grabbed her purse tight and scooched toward the door.

"I may be a lot of things, but I would never take advantage of this community. They helped my family when we had nothing, and I mean *nothing*. Everything I do is to provide, not take away."

T.J. stepped on the gas and the engine roared as he took off. He was driving fast down the road, causing the ride to be more violent than on the way to Mr. White's. Sydney held onto the door handle and tried with all her might not to bounce around the cabin.

When the truck came to a stop at the end of the driveway, Sydney said, "I'm sorry. I shouldn't have said that. Despite you being competitive, you've been nice to me, and if I don't get this deal, it's because you had the better pitch."

T.J. nodded. "Thank you. I'm sorry for the way I acted. I just—" T.J. looked at the clock. "You hungry?"

"I still haven't eaten my muffins." Sydney held up her to-go bag from the diner.

"I'll take that as a yes."

4

Marty's Pizza Palace

"T.J.! How's my best customer?" The patrons groaned. "Hey, when ya'll come here for lunch every day for years I'll call you my best customers too." They all immediately turned their heads back to their food.

"You came here for lunch in high school?" Sydney asked.

"I could only come if I brought admin back a slice of pizza." T.J. turned toward Marty and explained, "Well, Marty, I have a problem."

"As long as that problem is food-related, then I've got the answer."

"That's what I wanted to hear. This here," T.J. said, pointing to Sydney, "is Sydney, and she insists she's already had the best pizza ever."

"Is that so?" Marty crossed his arms and did his best to look angry, but his smile failed to hide his poker face.

T.J. glanced at Sydney, whose mouth was wide open and eyes were as wide as Marty's pizza pans.

"Let me close that for you." T.J. reached over, gently pushed up on her chin, and answered, "Indeed. So, I was wondering if you wouldn't mind fixing us one of your famous half-and-halves."

"The best of two worlds!" Marty started to backpedal. Stopping at the end of the counter, he asked, "Do I have liberties with the toppings?"

"Don't you always?"

T.J. led Sydney to his favorite seat at the back of the restaurant. It was a small table for two but for many years it was just T.J. sitting alone. He took his usual seat against the wall so he could gaze out at the customers enjoying their feast.

"Let me guess. This is your table?"

"It is." T.J. waved for Sydney to take a seat.

"And who said chivalry is dead?" She pulled the chair out and took her seat. "So, what's the story here?"

"What do you mean?"

"I assume you brought me here to tell me a sob story."

T.J. looked around the restaurant. There wasn't an inch of it that didn't hold memories. The brass footrail gave him just enough lift to see over the counter when he was a kid. If it wasn't a busy day, it also allowed him to slide from one end of the counter to the other. Almost directly behind Sydney were the saloon doors leading to the kitchen — the kitchen he used to sneak into to steal pepperoni to keep his stomach from growling. Marty never caught the "Pepperoni Bandit" but then again, he always managed to look away just at the right time.

T.J. let out a laugh. "How about you tell me what you think the sob story is?"

Sydney took a deep breath and began analyzing the restaurant. "This could be fun." She tilted her head slightly and looked up at the ceiling. "Okay, you said this town helped you when your family had nothing." T.J. shook his head. "So, your mom was a waitress here. You came here every day when not in school and sat at this table until she finished her shift. When you weren't eating or doing homework, Marty was like a second father."

T.J. laughed and pointed at Sydney. "That's good. Very good."

"So good that it's right?"

"No. I was the worker here. I was Marty's go-to guy when he was short-staffed. I did come here every day for lunch during high school, but it was always just to pick up. I've kept that tradition since graduating but other than that it's just full of great personal memories."

"Hey T.J.," a chipper voice called out.

T.J. looked up to see his high school sweetheart. "Sally, when did you get back in town?" He rose and the two hugged each other as if they'd not seen each other in years.

"Last night. I've been going around seeing everyone and I figured you'd be here." Sally looked around, taking in the whole scene. "This place hasn't changed, has it?"

"Thankfully." T.J. looked at Sydney, who was grinning from ear to ear. "Sorry. Sally, this is Sydney. Sydney this is Sally."

"Nice to meet you." Sally held her arm close as she waved.

"And you also. How do you know T.J.?" Sydney asked.

"Well, we grew up together and dated for a bit." She

turned her focus back to T.J. "Speaking of which I will let you two get back to yours."

"Oh, this isn't a date. This is strictly business," Sydney insisted.

Sally paused and smiled at T.J. "Working together or against?"

"Against," Sydney answered.

"Well, may the almighty have mercy on your soul. T.J. is one heck of a businessman, and in the end, you think you've won, but in reality, T.J. was the winner." The way Sally smiled and looked at T.J. was as if the spark they once shared had never left or at the very least was reignited. "Take it easy on her, okay?"

"I'll try."

Sally bent over toward Sydney. "Seriously, may there be mercy. This guy is amazing but savage when it comes to business."

T.J. rolled his eyes. "You know I can hear you, right?"

"Yes, and you know I'm right." Sally reached over and hugged T.J. once more. "I'll see you before I leave."

"You better."

"Sydney, great to meet you, and good luck."

She responded with, "You also, and thanks." T.J. took his seat and watched Sally leave. "Someone's got a crush."

"What?" T.J. snapped his head toward Sydney. "What are you talking about?"

"You both are still into each other. Whatever you both had is still there," Sydney explained.

"Even if that were true, which it's not, she's engaged and lives on the other coast."

"I didn't see a ring on her finger. Trouble in paradise, perhaps? She could be back to make moving arrangements."

"Sally isn't the type of girl you give a ring to. She's into more practical gifts."

"An engagement ring is a symbol."

"A symbol of spending a lot of money. People in this town focus on living, and a ring takes away from living."

"But that ring is the start of a new chapter," Sydney insisted.

"A positive or negative chapter? You see, let's just say that the ring costs a thousand dollars." Sydney sat back in her chair and curled her lip as though she smelled rotting meat. "Around here a thousand dollars could pay your car payment for several months, fix the broken fan belt, pay rent for another couple of months, and the list goes on. Yes, people here have luxuries, but they also believe in being practical. A ring that sits on your figure isn't practical for most."

"So, you're telling me that I won't find a single woman here that has an engagement ring?"

"No, I'm not saying that. There are just many who don't because they have other perspectives and responsibilities."

"So, what shaped Sally's perspective? She's well-dressed and kempt, which means she's probably successful."

"She's doing very well for herself. She moved after college and is a successful lawyer, but she grew up with nothing. Her father was an abusive drunk who ran off when she was in high school. The house she lived in was more like a shack and became such a health hazard that it was beyond hope of restoration; it had to be burned while she was at college."

"You still like her," Sydney persisted.

Marty interrupted their conversation, holding a pan on each arm. "Okay, my friends. Here we go." He slid one to Sydney and the other to T.J. "Half Stromboli stuffed full of meat, and the other half is pizza topped just with cheese. I'll be right back with a pitcher of Pepsi."

"Thanks, Marty," said T.J.

"Yes, thank you. This looks delicious," Sydney pulled her plate close and bent over to savor the smell. "I'm not sure I can eat all of this."

"Probably won't." T.J. grabbed his fork and knife and began cutting into the Stromboli.

"Here you go," Marty said, placing two ice-filled glasses and a pitcher on the table. "Enjoy."

T.J. had a mouthful and gave a thumbs up while Sydney replied, "Thank you." Marty left for the kitchen and Sydney peered over her shoulder to see if he was out of sight. "Since you're eager to tell me everyone's story, tell me Marty's."

T.J. swallowed and filled their glasses. After a sip, he answered, "Marty's grandfather moved here from Italy. He opened this restaurant shortly after and it has been operating ever since."

"That's all?" T.J. nodded. "There's no tale of heartbreak, struggle, and triumph?"

"Nope, just a family who worked their butts off." T.J. wrapped a strand of cheese around his fork. "You do realize that I'm not telling you these things so you won't build here, right?"

Sydney covered her mouth and shook her head as she chewed. After she swallowed, she asked, "So you're not going to buy all the land I'm trying to?"

"Oh, I am, and I will. Building a resort is fine by me, but not the park and shopping plaza. They're going to be what drives people out of business. Your guests may venture out, but it won't be many or often."

"So then, why are we here now? Me and you. What's the point? There's no way we're not going to build it all. Christmas Town is not enough to draw people in. Homemade goods are cute, but we're going to offer goods from all over the world. It will give people a chance to get things they wouldn't have a chance of obtaining otherwise."

"Here's the check and a couple of boxes to go." Marty placed the boxes on the table next to them and then handed T.J. the check. "I gave you the friends and family discount."

"You're too good to me Marty." T.J. wiped his hands on the napkin and grabbed the check.

"This one is on me. I can't be in debt to the competition." Sydney snatched the check from T.J. while Marty walked out laughing. Sydney almost spat out her drink when reading the tab. "How's almost seventy dollars a discount?" The kitchen filled with Marty's laughter and clapping.

"Turn it over," T.J. instructed. Sydney turned it over and examined the bill. "He does it to new customers and me on most days."

Sydney shook her head and mumbled, "Cute." She turned her shoulder and yelled, "Good one Marty." Sydney turned back to T.J. and asked, "So, why all this?"

"Honestly, I was hoping I'd be able to convince you not to build."

"And now?"

"I don't think I'm going to be able to change your mind."

Sydney grinned like the Joker. "I'm happy to hear that. After the past few hours, I didn't think you would give up, but—"

T.J. waved his fork and interjected, "But I haven't quit. I've just realized that this will require me to dig deep."

"I think my pockets run deeper than yours," Sydney gloated.

"They do." T.J. grabbed the to-go box and shoved his food inside. "I guess you've missed the point of what I tried to show you today."

"I didn't miss anything. Businesses come and go all the time, but our resort and parks will bring more jobs than those of this community could ever provide. We'll offer competitive pay, insurance, and retirement. Three things these mom-and-pop shops don't offer. Your community will finally not have to work until they die."

"I must say that you make great points and have a compelling argument." T.J. rose from the table. "When you pay, tell them to round up, please."

Sydney looked at the bill. "What does round up mean? You said that at the diner too."

"We have a going green initiative here. All the proceeds made from rounding up to the nearest dollar go to providing solar energy to lower-income families. It helps take one worry off their shoulders."

"How many families has this helped?"

"Only three homes so far. We started with the schools but once that project was complete, we decided to help low-income homes. We hope to add up to six homes by the end of next year, but we'll see."

Sydney grinned and turned away from T.J. He knew the smile

came with a budding plan. A plan that she was more than capable of fulfilling.

Sydney reached into her purse and pulled out a card. "Call me when you're ready to give up."

T.J. grabbed the card and looked it over. He tapped it on his pizza box and asked, "You don't want a lift to your car?"

"Thanks, but it's not far and it will give me a chance to see the town."

T.J. nodded and waved. "I'll see you around."

5

Sydney and Marty

"I thought he'd never leave." Marty sat across from Sydney. Beaming with anticipation he asked, "So how was it?"

"I've got to say that it is the best pizza I've ever had."

Marty slapped the table and shouted, "I knew it."

"Can I ask you something?" Marty waved his hand for her to continue. "Do you know why I'm here?"

"Hah," Marty scoffed. He leaned back and opened his arms wide. "Who doesn't?"

"You've been here a long time, right?" Marty nodded. "What do you think of our plans?"

Marty took a deep breath and avoided eye contact for a moment. "I wish I could say I'm happy with it, but I'm worried."

"Are you afraid we'll put you out of business?"

"No, I've got one foot out the door as it is. The odds are that by the time your place is up and running, this place will have new management." Marty started to look around and his eyes began to glaze over.

"I don't mean to pry, but are you selling out?"

"I've already sold, but it's not because things are bad. These old bones need a break, but I wasn't ready to quit and retire, so I found an owner willing to make a deal."

"What kind of deal was it?" Marty squinted at the question. "If you don't mind me asking."

"Nothing juicy. It's just that I'd work and run things until I'm ready to go."

"Why are you worried if there's no threat to your business?"

"Because when big businesses take over it's the people who work for them that suffer. I heard what you told T.J. about the perks, but you're missing a piece of the puzzle."

"What's that?"

"You see the young lady at the register?" Sydney turned around to see a woman in her mid to late twenties taking a call. "She called out six times this month. Based on that alone, what would you do to her?"

"Considering we're just halfway through the month, she would be fired."

"That's it? You would just fire her?" Sydney nodded. "That's Jessica, a widow with a four-year-old who's been in and out of the hospital lately. Nothing life-threatening, but serious enough for her to miss work. When she can't find a sitter, she makes deliveries instead of working behind the counter. We care about people here and don't throw them to the side when they don't follow a corporate checklist."

"I get what you're saying but we can't run a resort by letting thousands of employees come and go as they please."

"I understand, and that's why I'm worried. It's why T.J. is worried as well. His family has been here for a bit, but in the grand scheme of things they are new to the community. However, the way he's helped this place you would swear his family was a part of its founding. He knows that small-town business needs a personal touch, and right now it's a touch you're missing."

"Maybe I need to spend more time with T.J. and see how I can learn."

"Wouldn't be a bad idea. He's a good guy."

Sydney leaned forward and whispered, "What's his real name?"

"If he hasn't told you, then he has his reasons, and I won't betray that."

"I like you, Marty."

"Of course, you do. Everyone does."

6

T.J. and Mr. White (A Few Hours Ago)

"I hope you came prepared with a good offer." Mr. White extended his hand.

T.J. shook his hand; it was aged by a life of toil. "I think I got something you're going to like."

"Come on in." Mr. White led T.J. to the living room where they sat in beat-up recliners. "Let me have it."

"I know you want to go to assisted living and don't have the money. I also know that Sydney just offered you a small fortune."

"She's a firecracker. I like her."

T.J. smiled. "Me too, but I know her deal is just money, and you want more than that."

"Do I?"

"Your family helped start it all here, but if you sell out

to outsiders, then it's going to be like you were never here." Mr. White looked away and placed his hand under his nose. "Let me turn this into a museum and preserve your history."

Mr. White did all he could to conceal his sorrow, but tears were forming. "How?"

"I mean no offense when I tell you this, but the house and barn are beyond repair."

"I tried T.J. but I couldn't—"

"Mr. White, you don't need to explain anything. Life happened and you got the short end of the stick, but let me help. We can rebuild this place using all the materials that can be salvaged. The barn and the house will be turned into a bed and breakfast. I'll have your family pictures and coffee table books with your history spread throughout. Every person who comes through here will see what the White family did."

"But what about the living facility? I can't afford to stay there."

"I'll pay you what the land is worth and look into renting out the land but all that will go straight to you to make sure you'll be well cared for."

"What will happen to the land after I'm gone? Will you continue to rent it or sell it off?"

"I can't promise you that because I haven't thought that far ahead."

Mr. White laughed, then started to cough. "I refuse to believe you've not thought that far ahead."

"This time it's the truth." T.J. moved to the edge of the seat. "Mr. White, I'm not too proud to beg for help and I'm begging you now. This resort will change our community forever and

I'm going to do all I can to prevent our friends and family—" T.J. sat back in his seat. "my family— from losing it all."

"The moment I read the headlines I immediately saw a ghost town. I can see why you're worried about Christmas Town. I'd hate to see it close." Mr. White rose from the chair and walked to the window. "Do you promise to rebuild it like it was?"

"I promise that I'll take a few liberties and bring it up to date, but the bones of the house will be the same. We will reuse all that we can so that your family's legacy will live on."

"You got a deal on two conditions."

"I'm all ears."

"You do all the paperwork and don't say anything to Ms. Garcia. I'll call her first thing in the morning to let her know. It's best if I tell her."

"Done and done." T.J. walked over and shook Mr. White's hand again, finalizing Christmas Town's future.

7

Tensions Mount

"You son of a—" Sydney, along with everyone in the diner, stopped. She moved closer to T.J. "You knew, didn't you?"

"Knew what?" T.J. asked.

"Yesterday. You knew that Mr. White wasn't going to sell to me."

"No. I got the call this morning, and I'm assuming you did as well."

"Of course, I did. Why do you think I'm so mad today and not yesterday?"

"Why don't you have a seat and lower your voice by a hundred decibels?" The chair screeched along the floor as Sydney pulled it back. "You have to understand—"

"No, you need to understand that this resort will bring life back to this community and it will happen regardless of how many deals you block."

T.J. cleared his throat and became stone-faced. His voice deepened as he asked, "Why did you pick the border of Carrell County? Not only did you buy on the border, but you picked an area just miles from Christmas Town. Henry County has plenty of land to the northeast, but you picked land directly beside us, and then to add insult, you go after land in Carrell. Why?"

"What matters is that this is happening and the only thing you will accomplish is going broke."

T.J. leaned back in his chair, covered his mouth, and gasped, "I missed it." T.J. grabbed the paper, a pen, and started drawing. "I missed the end game."

"What are you talking about?"

"Not only do you not care about this town, but your goal is to run Christmas Town to the ground by suffocating it. It's why you chose properties on the border and why you want to buy in Carrell. This isn't the project you prove yourself but it's your project. You're behind the whole thing, not your father. You designed it all. The resort, the park, and the plan are all yours."

"It's not like that," Sydney insisted.

"Then tell me I'm wrong. Tell me you don't want Christmas Town to close."

Sydney turned and looked around at all the glaring eyes. "Perhaps this conversation would be better in private."

"You started it. I was just sitting here waiting for the check."

"Can we go outside?" Sydney asked.

"Why not stay here? Let the people know what you're trying to do."

"I'm going outside. You can stay here and sulk or come outside and let me explain it all."

Sydney left and T.J. sat there looking out at the eyes of all the townspeople staring at him.

"Everything okay?" Teresa asked. "Christmas Town isn't going to close, is it?"

T.J. slowly stood up and announced, "Sorry, everyone. I didn't mean for ya'll to hear that, but I'm going to do everything I can to keep Christmas Town open."

"If you need anything T.J. you just let us know," a voice shouted from the far end.

"Thank you all, but all I want you to do now is get back to enjoying your meal and the rest of the morning."

even going to put a canal weaving throughout the properties with gondolas."

"But—"

"But 'the people.'" Sydney raised her fists under her eyes mimicking crying. "This is going to be the last time I tell you and the last time you mention the people of the community. They will be well taken care of, and I'll give the main street the makeover it deserves once all of these mom-and-pops go under. Quit now or you'll lose everything to me when your only move left is to sell out." Sydney turned and walked toward her car.

T.J. watched her get in and drive away. Standing alone, he removed his phone from his pocket and hit the call button. "Uncle Jon, you got a minute?"

"Not really," he grunted. "I'm a bit busy here. Can I call you back?"

"I need to meet with you and Aunt Beth."

A bang thundered in T.J.'s ear. "Can you give me an hour?"

"An hour works. See you at the homestead."

9

Sydney Calls Home (Yesterday)

"Hello?" the deep raspy voice asked.

"Hello? Is that how you greet your favorite daughter?" Sydney asked.

"Sydney, I'm sorry!" The raspy voice of an aggravated businessman changed to a father's delight and rose an octave. "Your name didn't come up on the phone. How's the trip going?"

"Good and challenging."

"Been there." Juan chuckled.

"Which is why I'm calling. I need some advice on how to deal with one of the locals."

"Well, I've certainly had a lot of experience in that area, but I must say that every locality is different, so I'll offer what I can."

"I met this guy who is extremely knowledgeable about

the people and the area. He's even been somewhat helpful but he's also going after one of the properties I want."

"Do you think he'll get it?"

"Honestly, I do, but this is a crucial piece of land that will make everything go smoothly."

"What's the worst that could happen if you don't get this lot?" Juan asked.

"I'll have to try to buy others, but it could mean a bit of a redesign."

"The redesign would just mean a small delay, which isn't a problem. The problem is land. Are there more options?"

"There are, but what if this guy goes after them?"

"Do you know who this guy is?"

"Only his nickname. He won't tell me his real name. Believe it or not, I'm waiting in his car while he talks with the owner of the land I'm trying to buy."

"Have you checked his glovebox?"

"No. Why would I?"

"Check his glovebox, find the registration, and check the name on it."

Sydney grabbed the glovebox lever and pulled up. Nothing happened. "It's locked."

"Center console."

Sydney lifted the armrest and peered inside the compartment. "Nothing in here."

"I suggest finding out who this guy is before you buy anything else. You need to find out how far he's willing to go."

"What if he has a lot of money to burn?"

"Go scout properties that fit within the realm of what you can use, but aren't exactly interested in. Let him waste his resources on land that isn't essential to your goal."

"What happens if I buy non-essential land?"

"We're projected to have the entire project paid in full within a decade. I'm willing to spend what it takes and redesign what's necessary to secure this deal. You have my blessing to do what you have to do to make it all happen."

Sydney turned to look out the window. "I think he's coming. Got to go. Love you."

"Love you too, Princess."

10

Family Meeting: Part II

Since Sara's passing, her home has been converted into the headquarters for Christmas Town and a museum of the history of the business. Most of the rooms were converted into offices, the dining room became the meeting room, and dozens of other modifications were made to bring balance between a former home and a workspace.

T.J. walked into the meeting room where Beth and Jonathan were waiting. "Thanks for stopping everything."

Jonathan looked himself up and down. Dirt decorated most of his pants and shirt. "I'm okay with being inside for a bit."

"I take it that this isn't going to be a fun chat, is it?" Beth asked.

"Not at all." T.J. took a seat across the table from his aunt. His uncle took a seat at the head of the table. "I secured Mr. White's land."

"You did what!" Beth jumped up from the table. "How could you do that without talking to us?"

"It was with my money," T.J. explained.

"Oh." Beth took a seat.

"Despite it being your money, you should've consulted with us," Jonathan said. He leaned back, crossed his arms, and began rubbing his chin. "What was your plan?"

T.J. reached for a pad and pen that lay on the table. He drew a series of squares and rectangles and labeled them accordingly.

T.J. then pointed to each square and explained, "You have us, Mr. Hall, Mr. White, Mrs. Jefferson, the border between Carrell and Henry, and the land Garcia Entertainment bought. She can buy Mr. Hall's land, but it wouldn't mean much without Mr. White's property."

"There's no need bother to with Mrs. Jefferson's land when there are hundreds of acres between their other property that you don't own," Jonathan noted.

"Correct." T.J. pointed to his nose.

"Besides, Mrs. Jefferson owns at least a thousand acres. It would cost them millions. Right?" Beth looked at Jonathan for affirmation. "She could get upwards of five, maybe more."

"They have millions to spend."

"Okay, but at some point, they're going to run out of money."

"Unfortunately, they won't because the resort will be worth more than whatever investment they put into. I figured the best way to fight them would be to buy land to prevent expansion into Carrell."

"It makes sense that they would want adjoining land,

and buying Mr. White's property would prevent expansion," Jonathan noted.

"That's what I was thinking, but after speaking with Sydney I thought of something else." T.J. started scribbling more squares and names on the paper. "Beside Mrs. Jefferson are the Miller Estate and Wilson Farm that have a thousand acres combined. They are across from the Jones, Williams, Davis, and Moores of Henry County. That's just under eight hundred acres directly beside their already purchased land. They could buy all this and have more than enough."

Beth shook her head. "The paper said they only wanted eight hundred more. Why would they go after land in Carrell when they can get all the land they need in Henry County?"

"I have one theory and one fact. The fact involves Christmas Town. Christmas Town has put Fenton and Carrell County on the map."

"Though people may want to come to Christmas Town, when they search for us, they are sure to see the resort and change plans," Jonathan added.

T.J. pointed to his nose and then to his uncle. "The theory about the land revolved around the lower taxes in Carrell at first. However, the more time I spent with Sydney the more I believe it's about blocking us off. I think she wants to wall us off."

"What do you mean wall us off?" Beth asked.

"If she buys all the land around us, then it creates a wall or a buffer between us and them," T.J. explained.

Jonathan put his head on the table. "We'll be next door, but it will be like we don't exist."

"What do you think this means for Christmas Town?" Beth was fighting back tears.

"Honestly, with what we're competing against, I think we're looking at doing well for a couple of years, but it's going to slow down."

"Is there any reasoning with Sydney?" Jonathan asked.

"I don't think so. At this point, I believe she's counting on many of the businesses going under in Fenton so she can revamp the town."

"So how do we keep this place going? Jonathan, we can't let it go under. We can't let Mom down."

"I know, but I'm not sure what we can do. I'll talk with Dave and see what the finances look like. I know Mom's life insurance policy paid for a lot, but we still have some substantial bills."

"I'm almost tapped out. I promised Mr. White I'd renovate his home and turn it into a bed and breakfast so that's going to take a lot of what's left."

"So, you both think that if we pay off the bills then we stand a chance?" Beth asked.

Jonathan stood up and started pacing around. His frustration was obvious. "It's going to be hard to say, but it would give us some breathing room."

"Breathing room or life support?" T.J. asked.

"T.J.!" Beth snapped.

"I'm not happy about any of this, but we need to make more than just some business adjustments." T.J. looked at his uncle who waved to him to explain. "If we pay off all the debt before things get bad, it only means we'll own everything, which is great, but we could potentially own a ghost town."

Beth looked at Jonathan with wide eyes. "He's not wrong Beth. We may have to look at being proactive and see what's bringing in the least money and start closing."

Beth stood up and walked over to the pictures hanging on the wall. She touched the frame of one and asked, "Do you think we would have to shut everything down? I mean people will still be interested in cabin rentals. It will be cheaper to stay here than at the resort."

"So, I may have started us down the gloom and doom rabbit hole, but here is what I think we should do — Uncle Jon will talk to Dave about Christmas Town's accounts, I'm going to see about the finances of the restaurant, and Beth will keep things running here. We also need to look at personal expenses to see what the bare minimum is we can survive on. It's going to be in the best interest of Christmas Town if we cut our salary, so the employees won't suffer. But keep in mind that we may have to let some people go and pull more hours ourselves. It's unfortunate, but it will also give us more funds to pay off the debt."

"Agreed. I'll see if I can meet with Dave this afternoon." Jonathan looked at his watch. "How about we take a couple of days to gather all we can and then come back to the table here for a game plan?"

Beth nodded.

Instead of saying anything, T.J. got up and left.

11

Marty

Sydney poked her head through the door of Marty's Pizza when the door's chime rang out. She winced, and the hope of sneaking in vanished. Sydney pushed the door fully open and walked in to find an empty restaurant.

"Ah, if it's not public enemy number one," Marty yelled, coming into view.

Sydney stopped walking and asked, "Should I go or is it okay to stay?"

"Stay, stay. I was just teasing," Marty pleaded. He made his way to the counter where he met Sydney.

"Are you sure?" She sat her purse down and propped her foot on the railing. "I feel like I've got a target on my back."

"It's fine, and yes you do. Word of your display at the diner has spread like wildfire."

"Which is why I don't want to bother. People see me here and they may go somewhere else."

"My lunch rush is over, and besides, that would fall into your plan, wouldn't it?" Marty tried to squint and glare but his chuckle betrayed him. "I'm too old to care what people say."

"I'm glad because this may be the only place I eat for the rest of my stay." She looked outside. "You do know that I don't want people to lose their jobs, right?"

"And yet you know that some will be lost."

"I do, but I want to bring life back into this community. I want it to thrive," Sydney explained.

"Thrive under your ownership you mean." Marty turned and reached for a glass. "That's why you're here right? You picked Fenton because you can mold it to your image."

"You want the truth or white lie?"

"The truth would be nice." Marty pulled up a full glass and pushed it to Sydney.

"Thank you." She took a sip. "When I first heard of this area, I immediately thought I could turn this into the next Vail. When I first visited, I knew that's exactly what I could do." Sydney looked out the front window and pointed. "There is so much potential here."

"Why is it that your vision includes going after the businesses already here?"

Sydney sighed. "It didn't start that way, but the more I started to plan, the more I realized it was going to happen. The clients that we'll bring in aren't going to want 3D-printed or resin ornaments. They're going to want imported crafts made by tradesmen who carry on a three-hundred-year-old artistry tradition. They're going to want to eat at fine dining."

"Hey now!" Marty took a step back and opened his arms. "What do you call this if not fine dining?"

"You truly have amazing food, but look." Sydney turned to the seating area. "You are cramped, and the building next door is empty. Knock out that wall and create large booths. Add more tables and lighting but keep a soft white glow, and some creativity with murals. It's something little but will mean a lot."

"I like your idea and it's one that I've always had but the risk is too great for me to take."

"Too great? We could double your monthly income with just a small investment," Sydney explained.

"I like you, but I'm almost retired, and that's a project I don't want to take on. I'll let the owner take on that idea."

Sydney sauntered back to the counter. "Would you mind if I became the owner?"

"You would have to take it up with the owner and I can guarantee he won't sell." Marty looked past Sydney and stared blankly at the wall. He shook his head. "At the very least he'll make you pay an ungodly sum."

Sydney beamed with hope. "Who is this mystery owner?"

Marty looked to his right and then to his left. He leaned toward Sydney and whispered, "You'll find out soon enough."

Sydney laughed and pointed at Marty. "That was good. Okay, so I have another question that I think you'll be able to answer if you're up for it."

"Oh, I know I'll have the answer, but am I going to reveal it is the real question."

"What's T.J.'s story?"

Marty tapped his fingers on the counter and bounced his head back and forth. "Okay. I'll tell you if you answer one simple question for me."

"Deal."

"Deal?" Sydney nodded. "Is your interest in T.J. strictly business or personal?"

Sydney almost spat out her drink. "That's a difficult question."

"It's an easy question that you just answered."

"I didn't say a word."

"Your drink almost becoming mine is all I needed. If the answer were strictly business, then there wouldn't have been such an intense reaction or hesitation."

"It's difficult because I never rule out possibilities but our connection becoming personal isn't my intent." Sydney took another sip of her drink and waited for Marty to fulfill his end of the deal. However, he wasn't saying anything, so she urged, "Go on, spill it."

"Oh, yes. T.J. is the oldest grandchild of his family and the son of the youngest daughter. His mom was a sweet kid."

"Was?" Sydney asked.

"She's alive but was a bit of a wild child, especially compared to her siblings. T.J. came along during her senior year in high school, but she didn't want him. It's not like she hated or resented him, but she wasn't prepared to raise a kid. T.J. was primarily raised by his uncle Jon and grandmother, and they officially took over when she left. I think he was only two—" Marty nodded. "Let's call it two. He was two when she hit the road, but to be fair she was rarely around before then."

"That's one piece of the T.J. puzzle, but why is he so protective of the people here?"

"T.J. isn't a puzzle. What you see is what you get and what you get is the most caring person you'll ever meet. He cares like no one else here and that's hard to do because these people are some of the kindest and most generous people on Earth." Marty laughed but Sydney could tell it was to hide his pain. "You know that boy has only taken one vacation in his life."

Sydney's mouth dropped. She'd been on so many trips that she lost count. "You're kidding me? Only one?"

"T.J.'s family always took trips, but he never joined. Due to their business, there was always a need for someone to run things. When his grandmother left, he'd say he had to stay to help Jon. When Jon left, he'd say he had to stay to help his grandma. No one could get him to leave no matter what they tried."

"Do you know why?" Sydney asked.

"A couple of ideas have crossed my mind. One is that he wants to help and hates the idea of having fun while someone else is working hard. The other idea is just a theory, but I do know that was a fact."

"Go on," Sydney urged.

"I've always thought it was because of his mom. She rarely came around and I think T.J. was worried that if he left then he would miss one of her rare appearances. To him, a vacation wasn't worth the risk."

Any ounce of happiness or glee Sydney felt faded. Her shoulders slumped in a moment of realization. It's what T.J. was talking about. The stories are more than just stories. T.J.'s connection to this place and its people runs as thick as the blood that ties family.

"That's terrible."

"It's a theory, but I think it's a true one. I got to know T.J. very well and things he'd say from time to time have made me believe it to be true."

"So, what made him go on vacation?"

"His grandmother. She said that her greatest regret was not forcing him to be a kid. While other kids, including his cousins, played or went on vacations, he worked and learned the business." Marty looked up at the ceiling and took a deep breath. "She wasn't doing so well health-wise, and she begged him to not let her pass without going on vacation. His last Christmas gift was an all-expense paid trip to Europe."

"That's so sweet of her." Sydney's sorrow was starting to fade.

"He went, but while he was in Germany, they had the worst blizzard in a hundred years or more. It delayed his coming home so much that his grandma passed before he could get back."

Sydney's hand flew to cover her mouth but not before screeching, "No!"

"Sadly, yes, and what makes it worse—"

"How could it be worse than that?" Sydney looked at Marty, but he was avoiding eye contact. A terrible thought came to her and all she could say was, "No."

"Yes," Marty corrected.

"His mom came in for the funeral, didn't she?"

Marty looked away. Sydney could tell how much this was hurting him. "And was gone before T.J. got back."

Sydney placed her hand on Marty's, and in hopes to lighten the mood, she asked, "Why couldn't you lie to me?"

Marty laughed, and after a couple of sniffles, he explained, "Because the truth, no matter how tough, must be swallowed. Knowing the truth means you'll understand why the people are scared, why they're panicking, and why they're going to want to fight this."

"But what about my truth? What about my story? Doesn't that count for something?" Sydney pleaded.

"T.J. and I have been showing you our truths, so maybe it's time for you to reveal yours. Maybe then we'll understand and maybe then we'll open up."

"Okay." Sydney took a deep breath. "Here goes—"

"Not to me." Marty reached into the pocket of his apron. He pulled out a receipt pad and pen and started writing.

"I thought you wanted to hear it."

"I do and I will." He tore off the receipt. "But he needs to hear it first."

12

A Day of Deals

T.J. knocked on the old wooden screen door. It took a few moments, but an elderly woman hobbled to the door. She beamed with childhood delight as she opened the door and ordered, "Come in. Come in."

"You're not busy?" T.J. asked.

"Doesn't matter if I am. I'll always make time for you." Mrs. Jefferson waved for T.J. to follow. "Would you like something to drink?"

"Do you have any tea?" T.J. followed her into the kitchen.

"Cold or hot?"

"Cold and sweet if you have it," T.J. answered.

"Coming up. Have a seat." She pointed to the chairs.

T.J. sat at the small table meant for two while Mrs. Jefferson got a glass from the cabinet. She then grabbed some ice from the freezer and the tea from the refrigerator.

"I'm sorry it's been so long." T.J. watched as she poured the tea into a cup.

"No need for apologies. You're a young man and awful busy these days." Mrs. Jefferson handed T.J. his drink. "You're trying to save Christmas Town after all."

"You've heard all of that, huh?"

"I may be old and confined to this house, but I still have my ways of finding out what's going on."

"I suppose you know why I'm here then?"

Mrs. Jefferson nodded. "You either want to make sure I don't sell out to the resort or sell to you."

"I wish I could deny it, but I can't. I also can't afford to buy either. I was hoping for a neighborly agreement on not to sell."

"Hold on." Mrs. Jefferson got up and left the kitchen.

T.J. took the opportunity to look at his phone and drink his tea. He checked several of the local social media pages and read the comments, the arguments. There were many in favor of the resort and just as many opposed it.

Sam said, "I work three jobs because no one can afford full-time workers. This park will be a godsend."

Sara Beth replied, "Your prayer is our plague. What will happen to our hotel? We can't compete with that!"

Eugene added, "Good pay. Benefits. Entertainment. Tax revenue. What's not to like? Bring it on."

"You shouldn't be looking at that," Mrs. Jefferson informed.

T.J. hit home on the phone and the feed disappeared. "I know, but it's hard not to. I'm torn over all of this."

"Let me ask you this. Do you think buying my land or not selling it is going to prevent the build?"

"I did, but not anymore. I'm solely focused on preserving Christmas Town."

"Makes sense. It seems as though they will try to wall you off."

T.J. nodded. "Glad I'm not the only one who can see it."

"I'm not certain how this situation between Christmas Town and the resort will pan out, but you don't have to worry about me selling out." Mrs. Jefferson handed T.J. the papers she retrieved.

"What's this?" T.J. picked up the papers and started reading.

T.J. was halfway through the first page when Mrs. Jefferson said, "I don't plan on going anywhere for a long time. Well, a few more years at least but when I'm gone this is all yours."

"Why? Why would you—"

"I want you to learn from my mistakes, from *our* mistakes. Warren and I worked our lives away. Each year we'd say that we'd start a family next year and when the next year came, we'd say the same. 'We'll start next year,' but we never did. I've got a lifetime of memories with a million smiles or more, but not having a kid is the only thing I regret. I have no one to pass anything on to."

"I still don't understand. This would—"

"Mean more work for you?" T.J. nodded. "Granted, Warren and I planned for a good retirement, but it would have dried up some time ago if I hadn't started leasing out the land. It's good money and I don't have to work."

"I like the idea of not having to do the work but—"

"But nothing. You've worked since the time you could walk, and I fear you'll keep working long after you're gone."

"I'm not certain it's possible to work from the grave."

"Oh, I'm certain that the spirit of T.J. will rise and work the land the moment he's laid to rest." Mrs. Jefferson tapped on the papers. "Use my land how you see fit but use it wisely. Use it so that it allows you to work less."

"Well, I do have an idea that may help but I don't have years to wait."

"The lease I currently have will run out next June. Come back to me at least ninety days before then with a plan and if I like it then we'll run with it."

"Will you indulge one last question?"

"One more. A thousand more. Ask all you like."

"Why did you pick me? Out of everyone in this town, why do I deserve it more?"

"Your grandma and I were close." She laughed at the thought. "As close as two hard-working farmers could be, but we did manage to meet once a month for coffee. We'd keep each other up to date with this and that and without fail you were always part of her stories. I knew a long time ago you have that Santa-like spirit and you'd be the one who'd use my land to benefit our community."

"I don't know what to say."

"Thank you would be a good start."

T.J. lowered his head and laughed. "Of course, thank you. I promise I'll do everything I can to make you proud."

"I know." Mrs. Jefferson turned to the clock. "Now, get out of here and get back to saving Christmas Town."

T.J. left, and once in his truck, he dialed Stuart.

"A&S Electric. This is Stu—why? This is my cell. Hey, T.J."

"That was weird."

"Yeah, sorry about that. I've been answering calls nonstop since the resort was announced."

"Don't you have someone to do that for you?"

"I do but these are buyers."

"Buyers?" T.J. asked. "Hard to believe there are that many people out there who want to buy a power plant."

"I know, right? Once the resort was announced people with deep pockets have been calling. Most don't know a thing about electricity, but they see the park as a cash machine."

"Will it be? I mean, for you?"

"Honestly, I don't know. We'll have to pump millions into expansion just to handle the park. I love my dad, but he was fine with getting by. He never planned."

"To his credit, the declining population hasn't given him much reason to."

"True, but I'm looking at figures from other theme parks and resorts and this could be big for us. Resorts run non-stop and a theme park truly never closes with the maintenance that occurs after hours. They will use more juice in one month than this region does in a year."

"Can you handle that?"

"Would we be talking if you thought we could handle it? We go way back, but we haven't talked in ages, so something's up if you're giving me a call. Now—" He paused and cleared his throat. "Don't get me wrong, it's great to hear from you, but what's rattling around in that brain of yours?"

"I may have an answer to your problems."

"Mine or *ours*?" Stuart asked.

"Exactly," T.J. answered. "Are you still interested in solar farming?"

"Of course, but it's been difficult to convince anyone to try it."

"Why's that?"

"Right now, it's because of the contract. I'm willing to take on the financial risk, but it means a minimal profit for the first couple of years for the landowner."

"How minimal and how many years exactly?"

"You can't quote me on this but it's just a couple hundred a month per acre. The years are dependent on the amount of land, but it could be between two to five years at that rate. The additional kicker is the owner has to provide upkeep of the land to make it easily accessible for us to clean and maintain. The problem is they can get more from the major produce corporations, and in some cases, they don't have to do work."

"Would you do a contract with yearly payout increments?"

"That could easily be done, and I can throw in some end-of-the-year bonuses as well if things go better than expected. I'd do almost anything to prevent selling out, but these companies and the banks are making it tough to say no."

"Would around two thousand acres be of interest to you?"

"Jesus—" The phone went silent. "How? What have you done?"

"I bought Mr. White's land, and if the agreement is good enough, then I'll have access to all of Mrs. Jefferson's land."

"What do you mean good enough?"

"I think we'd have to do better than a couple hundred per acre to convince her to switch lease agreements."

"Honestly, and once again you can't quote me, but I think we can come up with one heck of an agreement for her. We can start with White's land and draw up something for Mrs. Jefferson when we get close to her property."

"Call me when the paperwork is done."

13

Jonathan and the
Accountant

The moment Jonathan crossed the threshold of Dave's Accounting Firm, a hidden voice called out, "Jonathan is that you?"

Masking his voice with a much higher pitch he replied, "No!"

"Come on back," Dave instructed.

Jonathan walked across the small lobby and into Dave's office. Instead of being greeted by Dave's goofy smile, Jonathan was looking at Dave's backside bobbing up and down from behind his desk.

"Everything okay?" Jonathan asked. "Oh yeah. It's fine. Have a seat."

Jonathan took a seat. "Where's Amanda?"

Still hidden from view, Dave answered, "Yesterday was her last day. Something about going back to school and needing a break before she starts."

"Not like you to sound so unconcerned."

Dave popped up, turned his chair around to face Jonathan, and took a seat. "I know, but it's tough finding good help and Amanda was excellent help. Of course, I want the best for her and am glad she's going back to school, but I'm trying to distance myself so I'm not so upset."

"Makes sense." Jonathan cleared his throat. "So, tell me you got good news."

"I wish I did." Dave thumbed through the stack of folders on his desk. His fingers suddenly stopped and he pulled out a folder and opened it. He removed the top sheet and handed it to Jonathan. "I estimated two doomsday scenarios for you. You also have to remember we don't know all the details about this resort."

Jonathan looked at the paper and started looking at the numbers. "I know we need to prepare."

"I understand but I want you to understand that all of this is hypothetical." Jonathan nodded. "The sheet you have is the optimistic scenario of the doomsday plan. I think that you'll have three years before the resort is fully operational. I also projected a thirty-five percent increase in expenses because it's always tough to count on the fluctuation of the price of any good."

"I'm good with that. We're seeing some price increases now, so it's best to be safe, and if we come under, then we can put that in the win column."

Dave nodded. "However, I accounted for a twenty-percent drop in income because the resort is new, and people are going to want to try something different. I considered the debt you have from the cabins and the additional land. I then ran the numbers based on a yearly additional drop of ten percent after the initial twenty and figured that you would have profit for two years after the resort opening and break even for the third. Past that is when things go into the red."

"So, we could have five more years of profit." Jonathan rubbed his hand through his hair.

"Potentially. I'm not certain how exclusive the resort could be. If they allow people to enter without staying on resort property, your cabins could be a saving grace. I wanted to prepare you for the worst, so I didn't include that."

"That's reasonable." Jonathan waved his hand in a bring it on gesture. "Let's hear the pessimistic scenario."

Dave handed him another sheet. "This accounts for the resort's exclusivity. I cut cabin rentals in half for the first year and then yearly by twenty-five percent until there are no rentals. Given the same increase in expenses, I'm estimating you will have one good year once the parks are officially up and running."

"If I had tear ducts, I would cry. I mean, at least with the first scenario we could cut back and possibly make it."

"Possibly." Dave held up a finger. "The only way I see you having a chance is to cut back now and pay off as much debt as possible." Jonathan started to laugh. "Did I miss something?"

"That's what T.J. suggested."

"Well, he's always been a smart kid." Dave passed another sheet of paper across the desk. "I would suggest starting with the Christmas bonus for the employees. I know it's one of the many benefits you all offer but the bonuses add up to a month's payment on one of the loans."

"I know you're right, but that's going to be a major blow for people."

"What's worse—losing your bonus or losing your job? I know you don't want to do it, but it's not like you're pocketing the money."

"I know, but it's still going to hurt."

"The sooner you make the decision; the sooner they can prepare."

"You have any other ideas?" Jonathan asked.

"Well, I know you haven't planted the last few hundred acres yet, so I would suggest growing trees for timbering or renting for farming."

"There are some trees that could be close to harvest by the time we need it in the optimistic scenario, but renting would be best for the pessimistic approach."

"Other than those, there aren't too many more options that would bring major cash flow." Dave closed the folder and leaned back in his chair. "If this resort were to never happen then there would be nothing wrong, but as it is, you've overextended."

"Well, we've talked about shutting down the attractions that make the least profit."

Dave shrugged his shoulders. "It could help but I think it's putting a Band-Aid over a dismemberment. Don't get me wrong, every little bit helps, but the money from the lack of electricity used is not enough savings. You'd have to cut employees who run them to make that move worthwhile."

"Well, that could be an option. We hire high school kids to help during the winter season, but the help will be missed."

"It may cause hours to increase for current employees, which may cause overtime pay to go up, but in the grand scheme of things, it could save thousands each season. Then again, if you close things the high school kids would run it may not hurt you at all."

Jonathan stood up and held out his hand. "Thanks for getting this done so quickly."

"Of course." Dave shook Jonathan's hand. "I know we're looking at the worst, but you need to try to stay as positive as possible. The resort may help us all more than what we realize."

"We can only hope."

"Works for me."

"I'll make all the arrangements but you're footing the bill since you asked me out."

"No problem."

"See you then."

****

The other end became silent, and Sydney hung up. The next couple of days were full of meetings, getting bids from builders, and scouting for more land. When the time came to meet T.J., Sydney drove to Paul's Steak House and made her way inside. It resembled any other large multi-service cafeteria. Different food stations were all around the center and the smell of beef cooking overpowered the scents of all other items.

"How many?" the hostess asked.

"I'm here to meet T.J. in the banquet room."

"Oh, yes. Follow me, please."

The hostess escorted Sydney to the back of the dining area. Sydney was met with a host of glares and stares from everyone she passed. They began to whisper, and though she couldn't make out what they were saying, Sydney knew it was nothing good and all about her.

The hostess pulled back a sound barrier. "Here you go."

"Thank you." Sydney moved past and saw T.J. sitting in the middle of the room.

"Hope this is okay." T.J. waved for Sydney to join.

She walked over to T.J. and caught a glimpse at the

serving table. "This will do, but perhaps the mountain of steak is a bit much."

"I know it's a bit overboard but there is a minimum requirement for the banquet room."

"What's the minimum?"

"Four types of meat, beans, mashed potatoes, and mac and cheese. Three pitchers each of water, sweet tea, and a soda. I think it's enough for like twenty."

"That's too much."

"I've not eaten much today so I hope to put a dent in it all. Besides, you can ask them to donate the leftovers to the food shelter. By tomorrow night the only thing left of this feast will be the aluminum pans."

"Oh, that will be great."

"Indeed." T.J. stood up and moved to the serving station. He grabbed a plate and held it out.

Sydney walked over and took the plate. "What do you recommend?"

"One of each. The steak, tenders, chicken breast, and ham are the best around. Hold off on the sides for the moment. The potatoes are from a box, and though they're good, they're not as good as the real deal. Beans are the same, except from a can."

"What about the mac and cheese?"

"Too much mac and not enough cheese in my opinion."

Sydney used the tongs and began adding the main items to her plate. "Why have the best meats around but serve mediocre sides?"

"All the sides used to be homemade or made from scratch or whatever you want to call it. The problem became the amount of waste and cost. Paul noticed when cleaning plates that the only items being thrown away were the sides. When the price of beef and pork rose, Paul knew raising the prices of dinner would hurt business. Box potatoes and canned beans were far cheaper than the raw ingredients, so he decided to offset the cost with inferior sides."

"So, he sacrificed quality to offset costs?"

"You can look at it that way, but the sides are just a cameo in the attraction that is called dinner. The stars are the meats."

Sydney followed T.J. back to their table where she examined her meal. "I like the cameo and stars analogy." She started to laugh as she cut into her steak.

"What's so funny?"

"This place is refreshing." Sydney smiled at T.J.

"I'm not following." T.J. shoved a large slice of steak into his mouth.

"The joking about the food. The eating whatever you want. The laidback atmosphere. I'm just not used to it all."

"Oh," T.J. said between chewing. After swallowing he asked, "Would you like to talk business instead?"

"We do need to talk about that, but I'm curious about one thing."

"Go on," T.J. urged.

"Why did Marty sell out but still decide to work?"

"Did you ask him?"

"I did, and he pretty much said he's ready to go but isn't ready to leave."

"That's pretty much it. The rest of the story revolves around his kids not wanting to take over. One lives down south somewhere and the other I think in Texas, so they would have to quit everything and relocate just to take over."

"That's understandable. But why the sellout and not leave? Why the whole cryptic ready to go but not?"

"He wanted to make sure he had the right owner who wouldn't change the restaurant once he left. Marty just wants to see the legacy continue, even if it's not within the family."

Sydney leaned to T.J. and asked, "Who's the new owner?"

T.J. looked around, leaned toward Sydney, and asked, "Why are you whispering?"

Sydney leaned back in her chair, looked around, and replied, "Dramatic effect." She started to laugh. "Sorry, I forgot we were alone."

"It's okay, but since you're asking, that means Marty didn't tell you, and it means I won't either. There are some limits to what I'll say."

"Fair enough."

Sydney continued to make small talk while they ate. She genuinely wanted a fresh start with T.J. to ensure that at least half of tonight was enjoyable.

15

Parley: Part II

"I can't eat anymore." Sydney threw her napkin on the table.

T.J. wiped his mouth. "Same here." He cleared his throat. "So, why are we here?"

"I need to tell you the other half of my story. The real reason I want this resort."

"I'm all ears."

Sydney took a deep breath and exhaled. "For as long as I can remember, I've traveled all over the world. No matter where I stayed it just didn't seem right. Even now, it's hard to explain why but it just wasn't right. As a teen, I drew my resort based on what I wanted. I wanted a place that could house activities for all seasons while providing something for everyone even if skiing isn't their thing.

"The more I learned about business, the more I started to fine-tune my plan. I did thousands of hours of research. I took half a year and traveled all over the states to find a location. Once I had the plan and the location, I hired a designer to illustrate my vision and I presented a plan to my father. This resort and its parks may look like just a business deal, but this is my dream, and you of all people must understand that."

T.J. nodded. "I do, but I don't trust what this resort is going to do to this community."

"I get that, but I don't understand part of the mentality here." T.J. shook his head and squinted his eyes. "You act like this is a community of a thousand people, but the county is home to almost thirty thousand residents. Despite having some major business chains here, everyone acts like you're just mom-and-pop shops."

T.J laughed. "Sorry, I don't mean to laugh." He sat up in his chair and scratched his head. "It's funny because it's true. I know we're a weird and protective bunch, but you've even said that you don't care if any of the businesses go under."

"Eh, I did say that didn't I?" T.J. smiled. "I even told Marty that he needs to expand."

"Just expand?"

"No. I shared my vision for the entire strip."

"Why did you pick here over anywhere else in America?"

"It's true that part of the reason is because of the key searches. The other part is due to land value and availability. The land in both counties is cheap and I can get loads of it without the concern of being landlocked."

"So, there's no talking you out of this?" T.J. asked.

Sydney shook her head. "No. I've bought more than enough land over the past couple of days."

"Can I ask how much?"

"An additional twelve hundred acres if you round up." T.J. hung his head down and avoided eye contact. "What's wrong?"

"I swear I thought I was good at business," T.J. said, looking up. "A couple of years ago I made one business deal that stretched me thin at the time but it's paying off now. Then I read the newspaper and hoped to block your buying of land. I thought you were going to try to suffocate Christmas Town."

Sydney shrugged. "To be fair, I was. I wanted to ensure it was landlocked and couldn't expand to compete with me."

"At least I was somewhat right, but I can't do it anymore."

Sydney leaned back in her chair and crossed her arms. "I didn't think you'd give up this easily."

T.J. sighed, and said, "Me either, but the problem is that I'm tapped out. There's nothing more I can do to prevent it from happening even if stopping it was a possibility."

"Did you know that almost twenty percent of this community is unemployed?"

"I did. We've got a task force trying to keep it from growing."

"Did you know that we could offer jobs to about two thousand of those unemployed? This is just based on our rough estimates. It may be even higher once the final plans are done. I wasn't lying when I said we'd offer benefits either. I do want people to be taken care of."

"You know you're going to have an extremely difficult time convincing the people."

"What if I have you in my corner? Come by my office and let me show you my plan."

"You've got an office?" T.J. asked.

"Well, no. It's just my room at the hotel, but all my plans are there, and I don't have a lot of choices until the on-site mobile office arrives."

"First you asked me to dinner and now you want me to come to your room. I'm all for being progressive but we technically haven't had our first date yet."

"We haven't?" Sydney extended both her arms and turned her head from side to side. "A catered dinner for two with sound-proof walls. How could one not consider this a date?"

T.J. snickered. "You haven't won me over yet."

"Does that mean you'll come to look at the plans?"

"Not tonight, but tomorrow. I got a couple of early calls to make in the morning, but I can stop by after that." T.J. paused and grinned. Sydney could tell the wheels were turning. "I just thought of something that may benefit you."

"How so?"

"How long are you planning on staying here?"

"From now until it is all up and running. This is my baby and I'll oversee all of it until I know it will be okay for me to leave, but I'll never truly be gone."

"So, like two or three years?" T.J. asked.

"I would say more like five. What are you getting at?"

"I know a house that is getting ready to go on the market. A nice two-bedroom log cabin located on twenty acres. It has all the comforts you need and plenty of space to work."

"Getting out of the motel would be wonderful, and the thought has crossed my mind. How much?"

"A million and a half." Sydney grabbed T.J.'s drink and started sniffing around the rim. "What are you doing?"

"Checking to see if you're drunk because that's too much."

"Do you have a better plan than the motel?"

Sydney shook her head. "I've got plenty of land but not the time to build if I want out of the motel as quickly as possible. I've looked into places to rent, and they wanted eight grand a month for a shack."

"So, it would be best to buy considering the cost of renting. Consider it just one more investment and one that would speak volumes to the community," T.J. informed.

"How so?"

"It would show that you're going to be here for a bit. Give the appearance that you're not just wanting to exploit the community."

Sydney squinted and her lips curled. Fearing it was another shack she asked, "Is it nice?

"It's five years old, has all the smart devices that one would want, and is cleaner than any motel you'd find." T.J. held up a finger. "Not that we have gross motels, but the owner has a weekly cleaning service come out to tidy up the place."

"Can you get me pictures first thing tomorrow? It's a lot of money but if it's a nice place, then we can get the deal done before the weekend is over."

"I'll do you one better than pictures. I'll talk with the owner and the realtor and see if we can get you over tomorrow morning."

"Sounds like a plan." Sydney stood up and pushed her chair in. "Are we good?"

"Oh no. You still have to pay the bill." T.J. moved from the table and stood beside Sydney.

"Yes, but I was talking about me and you."

"I do have a much better understanding of where you're coming from now."

"There's a but coming, isn't there?"

"But I haven't made up my mind yet. I'll review your plans and see what you have before deciding."

"Fair enough."

Sydney followed T.J. to the front counter where she paid off the tab, and the pair parted ways for the night.

16

For Sale

"Hello," Sydney answered.

"Sydney, it's T.J."

Sydney looked at her phone to check the time. "I thought you had some calls to make this morning."

"You do know that seven a.m. isn't early, right?"

"Only to you, it isn't." She sat up in her bed and rubbed her eyes. "What type of calls were you making on a Saturday before seven?"

"They weren't phone calls. House calls are more like it. There are a couple of shut-ins that I take food to on most Saturday mornings. They're early risers and so am I, so it works out."

"That's nice of you." Sydney yawned. "What time do you want to meet?"

"I'm heading over to the diner to pick up coffee and muffins. I'll be there to pick you up in about forty-five minutes."

"Sounds like a plan. See you soon."

Sydney got cleaned, dressed, and waited. She looked at the time. *It's been an hour. What's taking him so long? I could've slept longer if I had known this. And men say women are never on time.*

Sydney started to pace the floor. *Why are you nervous? It's just a house. Is this about the house? Damn that Marty. Why did he have to ask if it was business or pleasure?* Sydney stopped pacing and nodded. *Business. This is all business.*

A loud thud sounded three times from the door. Sydney stopped pacing and dashed to the table to get her purse. She rushed to the door, and instead of opening it immediately, Sydney paused, took a deep breath, and then opened it.

"Your chariot awaits Madam." T.J. stepped to the side, bowed, and motioned to his truck.

"Thank you, kind sir." Sydney locked her room door and walked to the chariot. She turned to T.J. who was making his way to the driver's side. "Shouldn't the chauffeur open the lady's door?"

"The shtick has to end sometime." T.J. looked at his watch. "And that time was ten seconds ago." Sydney rolled her eyes and got in the truck. T.J. followed and pointed to the center console. "Coffee and muffins."

"Thank you." Sydney grabbed a cup and a muffin from the bag. "How long of a drive is it?"

"Forty minutes give or take. It's on the eastern side of the county."

"That's what? Like an hour from my property? It would be a pretty far commute each day, don't you think?"

"How much experience do you have supervising construction sites?" T.J. asked.

"None."

"Then why would you have to go every day? Wouldn't a weekly, or even a biweekly, visit make more sense?"

Mid-chew, Sydney answered, "Good point."

"You're going to love it. The realtor is waiting at the house and the owner has signed all the papers."

After washing the muffin down with her coffee, Sydney said, "That's a bit presumptuous."

"Trust me when I say you're going to love it. As long as you keep the land mowed, then there is a clear view of the stream that runs at the back of the property from the deck."

"I like the sound of that." Sydney took a small bite and asked, "How do you know so much about this place?"

"I'm close to the owner."

"Oh, really? Maybe he'll be able to tell me your real name."

"He won't be there. I told you the papers are signed. You'll just need to do the same and talk to your bank."

"No need."

T.J. jerked his head toward Sydney. With an eyebrow raised, he asked, "No need for what?"

"Me dealing with my bank." Sydney tapped her purse. "I got the check ready to go."

"Thank god. I thought you weren't going to buy."

"As long as it's nice, I'll buy it. I need out of that motel and a proper office."

When T.J. pulled into the driveway, the realtor, Steven, was waving and grinning from ear to ear.

"He's excited," Sydney noted.

"For good reason. It is rare to have deals like this here. They typically only happen when someone passes and the family sells out or—"

"When a new business comes to town," Sydney interrupted.

"Exactly."

Steven rushed over to Sydney's door, opened it, and said, "A real pleasure Ms. Garcia. Unlike some—" He tilted his head toward T.J. incoming. "I think it's great what you're doing."

Sydney squinted and stared intently at Steven. "I can't tell if you're genuine or just sucking up."

"He's being one hundred percent honest," T.J. informed. "He's been trying to bring new business here for years."

"Now we have it." Steven looked at T.J. and grinned. It was one of not just delight, but victory. "So, tell me what you think of the outside?"

"It's a gorgeous spot, but how much does the upkeep of the grounds cost?"

"The price will vary, but currently my nephew's company does the grounds. I believe he charges the current owner two hundred a month, but as you can see," Steven held up his hand and twirled around, "he does an amazing job."

Sydney looked around at the grounds and nodded. "What about the exterior of the house? It looks brand new. Does he do that as well?"

"He does. It's power washed three times a year. Hard to believe a high school kid does this good of a job, but he's run his business since middle school, so perhaps it's a bit expected."

"That's impressive," Sydney said.

Steven clicked the garage door remote, and the door rose to expose a space large enough to fit two cars, as well as built-in storage on every wall. He gave them a tour of the modest A-frame cabin. It was as T.J. said: a two-bedroom, but the rooms were matching master suits. A half-bath was adjacent to the living room and a small breakfast nook rested off the kitchen.

"What do you think?" Steven asked.

"Who takes care of this place? I mean it looks like it was just built. The wood glistens like it was just polished. I understand having a house show ready, but I've never seen one in such impeccable condition."

"That would be my sister. I'm not sure how much she charges, but she and my nephew come here Saturday mornings."

"Okay," Sydney said.

"Okay?" Steven asked.

"You have a deal. Let's get the paperwork going so I can move in ASAP."

Sydney did all the paperwork needed, and when she finished she met T.J. outside. He was sitting on his tailgate with his legs swinging back and forth.

"All done," Sydney announced.

"Do you mind hanging out here for a few? I need to talk to Steven about some business."

"Sure. I'm going to walk around back and take a look at the stream you bragged about. Yell when you're ready to go."

"Will do." T.J. hopped off the tailgate and made his way inside.

17

Is it Business or Personal?

T.J. made his way to the living room and watched Sydney walk around the back through the windows. He continued to watch her as she made her way to the creek.

"You know what you're doing is the very definition of creepy," Steven informed.

"Only out of context. I just want to make sure she can't hear."

Steven walked up beside T.J. and asked, "When are you going to tell her?"

"Tell her what?"

"Oh, I don't know. How about your real name? Oh, oh, or even better, the fact that you just sold her your house."

T.J. shrugged his shoulders as he continued looking outside. "She'll find out eventually, but I had no choice."

"T.J." Steven placed his hand on his shoulder. "Are you okay?"

"I bit off more than I can chew, but selling the house will

pay off all I owe and the rest will go to Christmas Town. I can't see it go under."

"Is Christmas Town in trouble?"

"Not yet, but it will come to a point where we will be."

"Oh." Steven took a few steps back. "I didn't think about what the resort could do to Christmas Town. I was simply happy to hear about the jobs and the revenue that it will bring, but I didn't think about how it could hurt."

"Honestly, I could be worrying for nothing, and this resort brings a lot of business our way."

"But you can't take that chance."

"No, I can't. When grandma came here, she had nothing yet given me everything."

Steven cleared his throat. "That's where you're wrong. You earned everything you got from her. I mean, how many eight-year-olds worked at Christmas Town's bakery? I don't mean you sat there and looked cute, because we both know you weren't a cute kid; you baked for her, you completed orders, took the money, cleaned, cut grass, and the list goes on."

"You know what I mean. Selling this means I pay off Mr. White's land, the restaurant, and a good portion will go to Christmas Town."

"Speaking of restaurants... Does she know you bought out Marty?"

T.J. turned to Steven. "Not yet, so please don't say anything."

Steven held up the paperwork in his hand. "Your name and signature are all over there, but did I tell her? No."

"Laying it on a little thick, aren't you?"

"It's only as thick as that skull of yours."

T.J. laughed. "That's a good one."

"I'm not an expert at many things, but I can tell something is going on between you two."

Avoiding Steven, T.J. turned back to the window. "Nah, nothing's going on."

"What do you call it when a businessman helps out the person who could potentially run him out of business?" Steven didn't wait for a response. "Look, you are the most helpful person this town has probably ever seen, but helping her is more than just helping someone."

T.J. deeply inhaled and released his breath with a long, drawn-out exhale. "We had dinner last night and it was amazing. She was...I don't know. She was great to be with."

"Then ask her to go out tonight. Tell her everything before she finds out. If you hide too much you risk causing an irreparable rift."

"I'm no stranger to people not liking me."

"Um, yes you are. You've never made an enemy in your life and she's going to be around for a long time, so you better not make her one."

T.J. reached for his pocket and grabbed his keys. He unthreaded his house keys and turned back to Steven. "I'll leave the other garage door opener on the counter. I'll be out by Monday."

Steven grabbed the keys and asked, "Where are you staying?"

"There're a few cabins not being rented so I'm going to see if I can be a long-term tenant."

T.J. walked out the deck door and headed to the creek. He could see Sydney admiring the view. The same view he's loved for the past few years. He hated leaving the house and the land but knew it was for the best.

"How do you like it?" he asked.

She responded without peeling her eyes away from the natural landscape. "Like isn't the word. I *love* it. It's so peaceful here. All you hear is nature."

"Steven called the owner—they are going to work on being out by Monday."

"That's really quick. It's going to take some time for the paperwork to process."

"The owner knows who you are and is certain the check won't bounce." T.J. tapped her on the shoulder. "Come on. We have to hit the road."

"So soon?" Sydney whined.

"Don't worry. Before you know it, you'll have plenty of time to soak it all in."

They took the short walk to T.J.'s car and embarked on the even longer drive down the driveway.

"Can I ask you a question?" Sydney asked.

"As long as I reserve the right not to answer," T.J. replied.

"How is it that you became a trust fund kid?" T.J. chuckled and turned to Sydney. "What?"

He shook his head. "Nothing. It's a good question. As you know, I was raised pretty much by my uncle and grandma. I started working on the farm and the other family businesses when I was young, far too young to work. When I was around eight or so, I was old enough to help without getting in the way. My favorite thing was riding the mower. My grandmother wanted to pay me, but my uncle said no."

"That's terrible!" Sydney squealed.

"He believed I'd just waste the money on candy and junk, so they compromised and started a trust fund. They did this until I was sixteen, and then they gave me my mother's share of the business."

"Why did they wait until then?"

"I think it was because they hoped she'd come back. I was officially put on the company's payroll and the company share was placed into the trust. I got a small inheritance when she passed and that was added to the trust." T.J. felt Sydney's eyes on him. He turned toward her and saw a devilish grin. "What?"

"You're just not like the other guys I know."

"You mean other guys you know go broke trying to prevent you from moving in?" T.J. returned the grin with one of his own.

Sydney smiled as she brushed the hair. "They've never done that, and you're not broke."

"No, but I'm stupid."

"You're not. What you did is rarely seen anymore, but I did warn you."

"That you did."

There was an awkward silence between them. It was like that point on a first date where you want to talk but are unsure of what to say.

Sydney broke the tense silence. "When we get back to my room, would you like to come in and take a look at things?"

"Actually, I was thinking I could pick you up tonight. We could grab dinner, and then I could take a look after."

"Why after?"

"I'd like to have a pleasant dinner."

"Do you think seeing the plans will scare you that badly?"

"Ha," T.J. blurted out. He turned to Sydney. "Sorry, I just know it's going to be worse than I thought, or maybe it will be okay."

"Since the day I met you you've been pessimistic, so can you try to be a bit more optimistic tonight? I feel like we just keep going around and around. I say it will be okay." Sydney cleared her throat and mockingly grunted, "And then you say, 'No, it won't.'"

The impersonation was spot on and T.J. burst into laughter. "Okay, okay." His laughter subsided. "But in the interest of a fresh start, I need to come clean about some things tonight."

"Oh, T.J. has some secrets."

He nodded. "I do, and all will be revealed tonight."

"Today's just going to be filled with revelations, isn't it?"

"What do you mean?" T.J. asked.

"The county meeting. Don't you remember? It's this afternoon."

"Oh, I wasn't going to go to that."

"What? Why not?"

"As of now, you're not building in my county so none of us have a say. This meeting is just a formality to give people peace of mind."

"You know; I've never thought of it that way, but would you think about it? I could use a friendly face in the crowd."

"Even if that friendly face isn't really in your corner?"

Sydney put her hand on T.J.'s leg and the two locked eyes. "Please reconsider. I don't know how to say it without sounding corny, but here it goes. There's just something about you that makes me feel calmer, even with the frustration."

T.J. turned back attention back to the road. "I'll consider it."

Sydney pulled her hand back. "Thank you."

"You're welcome, and you can wipe that grin off your face."

"What grin?"

"I don't even have to look to know it's there."

The rest of the ride was quiet, and when they arrived at the motel Sydney said goodbye and walked to her room.

T.J. drove off and headed to Christmas Town.

18

Town Archives

"Greetings, Ms. Garcia."

The polite words came from the woman behind the checkout counter. She wore a red turtleneck, her hair was as black as the night, and she looked as though she could still be in college. She closed the book and placed it on the counter.

Sydney approached slowly and looked around before replying, "Hello, Ms.—"

"Watson, but you call me Lizzy, or Ms. Lizzy."

"I'm sorry, but have we met? Maybe at the diner or Marty's perhaps?"

Lizzy shook her head. "No, this is our first meeting, but you've become a bit of a celebrity around here."

"One that is more infamous than famous." Sydney looked at the book cover lying on the counter. The flame coming from the young woman's hand intrigued her. "Good book?"

"Very much so. The author puts a spin on witches, were-wolves, and vampires, and the protagonist is phenomenal. Loads of action, with no gory details spared, and the heroine isn't ruined by a love interest."

"I'll have to look into it when things calm down."

"Highly recommend it, but this is not what brings you in today, so how can I help?"

Sydney turned to her right and saw the children's section. To her left was the young adult section and just past that was a sign for adults. "I've been told you have a magnificent archive, but it doesn't appear to be easily found."

"We do. Follow me." Lizzy waved over her shoulder, a sign for Sydney to match her pace.

Lizzy walked around the counter and headed toward the young adult section. The stacks opened up to a seating area just past the adult section. Taking a sharp right turn, Lizzy led Sydney to an arch with Fenton Archives in gold lettering on the double doors. They entered a room that was at least double the size of the general collection.

"We are short-staffed today but if you need something specific press zero on the phone and it will connect you to the front desk." Lizzy pointed to the phone located on the farthest table. "Is there anything I could help you find for the moment, or do you want to browse?"

"I'm trying to find out who T.J. is and more about the history of Christmas Town." Lizzy's eyes widened. The look was not of shock but panic. "It's not what you think. I'm not stalking him, but we've been spending a lot of time together and I'm trying to learn about this town."

"I'm assuming that you mean to find out his real name?"

"I am. I've asked but he won't tell."

"I must say, I don't agree with going behind his back but you're sure to find what you're looking for here. I would suggest looking at Christmas Town's website for its history. There are thousands of articles on microfilm that may cause you to spend many days combing through. The metal cabinets on the left wall contain all the rolls if you wish to go that route."

"Would you happen to have a high school yearbook collection?"

"We have every one from each school since yearbooks were made. There's a section in the far back on the right. The stacks are labeled Carrell County Public Schools. As you do your research, please don't use pens if you need to write something down. There are pencils and paper on the table, and we monitor with cameras, so keep that in mind. Anything else you can think of?"

"Not at the moment, but I'll call if something comes to mind."

"I'll leave you to it then."

Just as Lizzy was taking her leave, Sydney yelled out, "Wait, there's one more thing."

Lizzy stopped and turned around, "Sure."

"I've tried to look up land records before moving here but there's nothing online. Do you have them here?"

Lizzy started to laugh. 'Forgive my reaction, but the county has neglected record keeping. They have all you need at the government centre, but public records are a mess. I wish they'd update them, but I doubt it will happen. If you want to know who owns land in this county, then it's best to talk to T.J. or

Steven. Keep in mind, Steven will only let you know about the land you're going to buy."

"Thank you."

"Anything else?"

"No, that's it for now."

Sydney placed her bag on the closest table and headed back to the right corner. There were five stacks dedicated to Carrell County Public Schools. The yearbooks were located on the very last stack and took up almost all the room. Sydney followed the years until she came to the most recent.

"I'm going to assume you're twenty-five so—" Sydney moved over a few years. "Let's start here and go back eight years."

She grabbed the stack and made her way to the table. Sydney started with the most recent volume and thumbed through the book's pages. Each flip revealed the exploits of young teenagers. Students were posing in the halls between classes, homecoming celebrations, and highlights from all the sports. The yearbook was just like any other, and it sent Sydney on a journey back through high school. Three girls were posing in the hall, but they weren't random. It was Sydney standing with her friends Sasha and Jessica. Sydney continued to replace the unknown faces with her memories but finished the first yearbook without finding T.J.

The next one ended with the same results. T.J. was nowhere to be found, that is until her third attempt. Finally, she found what she was looking for. The smile she had become fond of was on almost every page. It took a few pages before she found his name, but in black print, she read *Jonathan Cunningham*. She ran her index finger many times across the print.

She tapped her finger on the name. "Jonathan...Jonathan...Jonathan Cunningham. Why is your name so familiar?" Sydney leaned back in her chair and repeated, "Jonathan Cunningham. Why is your name so familiar?"

Like a bolt of lightning, Sydney shot up and dug through her purse. She found the black and grey business card that floated to the bottom. In bold white letters was Steven Becker Realty. Sydney grabbed her phone and dialed.

A chipper voice answered, "Steven Becker speaking."

"Steven, this is Sydney Garcia. Do you have a minute?"

"Absolutely. What can I do for you?"

"What was the owner's name of the house I just purchased?" There was a long silence. "Did I lose you? Steven?"

"No, I'm here. It— it was Jonathan Cunningham."

"I knew it. I knew I knew that name." Sydney sighed deeply. "But I wish I didn't."

"I take it you've figured it out?" Steven asked.

"I did, but why wouldn't T.J. want me to know it was his house? I joked about him going broke, but could he be going broke?"

"I have the answers, but I won't give them. There was a reason and I respect that, so I've got to tell you to ask him."

"We're going to have dinner tonight but—"

"But nothing. Go to dinner and let him explain why. Dig deeper and you're going to understand even more."

"You're right. Thanks."

Sydney hung up the phone and pulled out the tablet from her purse. She went to Christmas Town's website and searched each page for a reason T.J. would be so attached to the business.

The reason must be more than what Christmas Town has done for the community, but there wasn't a single picture nor mention of his name.

She found the names Sara and Jack spread throughout the website, but only one picture contained their names. All the others focused more on the event and joy of the moment than the individual. Though the pictures may have been to capture the moment, Sydney looked at everyone and couldn't find anyone resembling T.J.

Giving up hope, she picked up her phone and called her dad. "Why is it that I had to hear about the progress you're making from the project manager and not you?"

"Hey, Dad. I'm well. Thanks for asking. How are you?"

"Forgive me. You know I care about you, but I don't want to hear updates from the project manager. I want to hear them from you."

"I know, but things have gotten complicated, which is why I haven't updated you."

"Complicated?" Her father's sigh screeched through the phone's speaker, and she heard his chair squeak—he must have leaned back out of stress. "Complicated usually means something personal."

"There's nothing about this venture that isn't personal. There are many that object to the build and few who agree to it."

"Why are they objecting?"

"They fear Christmas Town will go under."

"Will it?" he asked.

"I don't know." Sydney closed her eyes and took a deep breath.

"That's not true. I'm certain it will close. They won't be able to compete with us."

"Before you left you were fine with doing what it takes. What's changed?"

Sydney took another deep breath to steady her nerves and leaned back in her chair, a coping mechanism she got from her dad. "There's this guy—"

"Ha! I knew it was personal."

"It's like that, but it's not like that."

"Let me guess. He doesn't want us to build, but you like him."

Sydney ruffled her hair. "He's different. He cares for this community more than anyone I've ever seen, but I don't know how I feel. I just know I wished I cared as much as he does."

"It's simple. You just start caring."

"It's not that simple," Sydney retorted.

"Why not?"

"Because I want this project," Sydney answered.

"Both are possible." A grunt and another squeak came from the speaker. "Do you remember my first secretary Maria?"

"Maria? Not really."

"You were young when she retired but she worked for me from the start of the company until you were five or six maybe. I was dead set on long hours, and that wasn't just for me but for her also. I got a call about this talented kid and was told he could be the next Elvis."

"Elvis? Are you sure this was when I was a kid?"

"Careful," her father warned. "I told her to book the next jet out and take the car to go home to get a bag. I went to do something, but when I went back to her desk, she was on the phone explaining to her kid that she wouldn't be able to go to her graduation. She was holding back tears."

"Please tell me you didn't make her go."

"I didn't. I gave her time off and an all-expenses paid vacation for herself and her family. I realized that while trying to build the company I was hurting the people that made it run. What I want you to understand is that we will be okay if this plan fails but the odds of failing will increase if you don't care about the people this will affect the most. Listen to this—"

"T.J.," Sydney cut in.

"Listen to this T.J. and see how you can have your vision and the people's as well."

"That should be easy since we're having dinner tonight, but I'm worried that if I have to change it won't be my vision anymore."

"Time is on our side, so don't rush into anything. Listen, plan, and then act."

"I will. I'll update you soon."

"You better."

Sydney pressed end and took the yearbooks back to the stacks where she found them. As she made her way back to the front desk, Sydney saw Lizzy engrossed in her book.

"Thanks for all your help today," Sydney said.

Jerking her head up, Lizzy replied, "Did you find what you were looking for?"

"Almost. Christmas Town doesn't have a lot of names listed in its history, so it wasn't much help and I didn't feel like combing through the microfilm."

"You could take the more personal approach." Sydney stared

at Lizzy as though she had grown a third eye. "Take a trip to Christmas Town and ask the owners about it. I'm sure they'd like to meet you, considering your plans."

"That's a good idea but I'm not sure they'd welcome me. I'm not afraid of confrontation in the board room, but I'm not sure I'd do well going there alone."

"Honestly. I'm sure there's some concern about the future of Christmas Town, but they will treat you like family."

Sydney grinned and asked, "So they'll treat me like family to my face but will threaten me behind my back?"

Lizzy nodded. "Probably, but what do you have to lose?"

"Good point." Sydney started to turn to walk away. "Thanks again for your help today."

"You're welcome. Enjoy the rest of the day."

19

County Meeting

T.J. walked into the high school gym, which was abuzz with hundreds of murmuring residents. Some were louder than others, but the gym was noisier than when one of the school's basketball games was taking place.

T.J. heard some saying, "Bring it on," and others pleading, "We have to stop it."

He walked past each row and looked for an empty seat but failed to find one. The last row opened to about ten feet of space. A small stage that rose two feet off the ground was set up with five chairs for the board of supervisors and a podium. With nowhere else to go, T.J. walked to the back of the gym and took a seat in the stands.

"Mind if I take a seat?"

T.J. looked over at Sydney. "I now have a strange sense of déjà vu."

Sydney stepped over the first row and took a seat beside T.J. "Thanks for coming."

"I figured the worst that could happen is that I get some entertainment out of it all. I mean, look at all of those friendly faces out there." T.J. looked out and saw a lot of death stares aimed at Sydney.

She nodded. "A whole lot. Who's that one with the trucker's hat?"

T.J. scanned for the trucker's hat. "Ah, Mrs. Thomasson. She drove a truck for just over thirty years and is a bus driver for the school."

"Why does it look like she wants to kill me?" Sydney asked.

"Because she does," T.J. answered. "And she could," he added.

"I'm sure, but why?"

"I could go ask if you want?"

"No, that's okay."

T.J. shrugged his shoulders. "The odds are she is one of the many who want this to remain a small community or a community that cares." T.J. looked at the folder resting on Sydney's lap. "That's one heck of a file there. You have at least ten sheets of paper for each person here."

Sydney tapped on the cover. "Let's call this the ace up my sleeve or the hail marry pass to win the people over."

T.J. looked to his right to see the board of supervisors entering the gym "Looks like we shall see if your receivers will make the catch."

Mr. Walsh stopped in front of Sydney and T.J. "Ms. Garcia, I'm George Walsh. I represent the second district."

"Nice to meet you."

"Please join us on stage."

Mr. Walsh held out his hand to help Sydney down, and without acknowledging T.J., they walked up to the stage. A chair was brought up for Sydney and the moment she sat down, T.J. saw her take out her phone. Seconds later he felt a buzz in his pocket. He pulled his phone out of his pocket and opened the message.

"Sorry about that. I didn't mean to rush off without saying anything."

T.J. replied, "It's fine. Mr. Walsh wants your resort more than anyone here and he's mad at me."

"Oh."

"Yep."

"Greetings, all," Mr., Walsh announced. "I, on behalf of the board, would like to thank everyone for coming out this evening. Before this meeting, we asked everyone who'd be attending to complete a survey stating their name and if they were for or against the resort. We took those names and placed them in a box." Mr. Walsh motioned at two of the board members, each of them holding a box. "We'll draw six people for and six people against to speak their minds for a total of five minutes each. After this, Ms. Garcia will speak to clarify many of the concerns that have been brought up. Those who have other concerns can email, call, or arrange a one-on-one meeting. However, please keep in mind that despite the land being purchased, the resort has not been approved by Henry County and we can only address the concerns and permits relating to Carrell."

For an hour, T.J. listened to those in favor and those opposed. Those opposed shared the same concerns as T.J. and his family. What's to become of the smaller shops when something seemingly better is available at either the resort or the theme park? Those in favor wanted jobs and benefits. It was the story of Jackson Bryant that started to change his mind about the resort. Jackson worked for the Henry Carrell Timbering Company (HCTC for short) since the time he was in high school. It went under three years ago, and due to the large number of people needing employment, jobs were hard to come by. He did all he could for work but struggled to provide for himself and his family.

Mr. Walsh took the mic once more. "Thank you to everyone for your cooperation. I would like to introduce you to Ms. Garcia, the proprietor of the resort."

Many clapped and cheered but just as many did nothing.

Sydney took over the podium and gazed across both sides of the stage. "Thank you, Mr. Walsh, and thank you to the board for hosting this." She refocused on the audience. "Thank you to those who voiced concerns and expressed support today. What I have to say will be brief and revolve around what I've been saying since I arrived. We're only looking to form a relationship with the people of Fenton. We'll provide well-paying jobs with a great benefits package that includes retirement for certain positions.

"I know many of you are concerned about your business. That's why I've brought this." Sydney held up her folder. "We'll need florists, landscapers, interior designers, and much more. All of which this community can provide."

Sydney was still talking when T.J. slowly got up and walked out of the gym. The meeting gave him the perspective he needed.

20

Dinner

T.J. knocked on the hotel door. The chain lock rattled and the deadbolt clanked as it receded into the door. The knob didn't turn, and Sydney didn't make a sound.

It caused T.J. some concern so he asked, "Is everything okay?"

The door slowly opened. Sydney wore a red, form-fitting dress and T.J. felt his jaw drop.

Sydney pointed to T.J.'s mouth. "I hope that's a good reaction."

"Of course." T.J. looked down at his blue collared shirt and tan khakis. "You look amazing, but I feel a bit underdressed."

"Or I could be overdressed." Sydney bit her lip and grinned.

"In a way, we balance each other out."

"Well said. Shall we?"

T.J. led Sydney to the truck, and they took off, making their way out of the town.

"Where are you going? All the restaurants are back that way." Sydney pointed to the back of the truck's cabin.

"I told you that there are some things I want to tell you, and I found the perfect place to do so."

"Will this be T.J. or Jonathan telling me?"

T.J. kept his eyes on the road but clenched his teeth. He nodded. Through clenched teeth, T.J. asked, "Who told you?"

"In a way, you did. You told me Fenton had an excellent town archive, so I visited it, looked at your yearbooks, and found you."

T.J. started to laugh. "Very clever and very embarrassing."

"Not to take away from moments that shouldn't have been photographed, but why all the secrecy? Why didn't you tell me your real name? Oh, perhaps most importantly, why did you sell your house?"

"I'm not sure if I'd call it secrecy, but I never expected to spend this much time with you. When I read the article and saw your picture, I thought you were just here to sign paperwork and you'd leave."

"It's odd, but I'm glad we've been able to spend so much time together."

T.J. turned to Sydney and saw that captivating smile. Had Sydney been anyone else, he would have never thought twice about asking her out properly. Instead of worrying about Christmas Town or business, his focus would be on making her laugh or creating memories. It would've been on anything but business.

"Me too," he replied.

"So, what about the house?" she pressed.

T.J. turned his focus back to the road. "I got in over my head. Honestly, I'm not sure if your resort is going to be good or bad for us, but I needed to pay off my business debt before a potential downturn."

"Are you going to share what your business is, or will it be another secret until I do more digging?" T.J. only laughed. "That's not an answer."

"I bought Marty's place." Sydney smacked him on the shoulder. "Ouch!"

"Why would you keep that from me?" she yelled.

"I guess it's because I want people to always see it as Marty's place and not mine."

"How do you do that?"

T.J. looked at Sydney and asked, "Do what?"

"You have this knack for making people feel bad instead of angry."

T.J. put on his turn signal. "I got that from my grandma." He made the turn into Christmas Town, but Sydney was none the wiser. When T.J. looked over, Sydney's eyes were fixed on him. "What?"

"Nothing," Sydney answered.

"So, you know how I told you that I had some things to explain tonight?" T.J. looked at Sydney and she nodded. "Well, you already pried one out of me but the other relates to all my other secrets and this place."

T.J. pointed out the window. The fading sun glistened across cabins and the faint glow of soft white lights outlined every building they passed. They followed the road past Santa's Village, the ice-skating rinks, and to the back of the property where T.J. parked the truck in front of a cabin.

"For the first time since we met, you're speechless," T.J. noted.

"This is Christmas Town, isn't it?" T.J. nodded. "Why did we come here? Have you talked to Lizzy?"

"I haven't, but this is my temporary home, and I've made you dinner." T.J. got out of the truck, walked over to Sydney's door, and opened it. "Come on. I promise all is going to be explained shortly."

Sydney was hesitant about getting out, and T.J. could see her once happy face was now sad. The smile was no longer there; her head hung low and her movements were slow. A simple turn to the side and step down that should have taken seconds became stuck in time. T.J. led the way as he tugged her along.

He opened the door and bowed, "After you."

Sydney's sorrow quickly faded as she played along and curtsied. "Such a gentleman."

T.J. followed Sydney and closed the door. The cabin was fully furnished but was a model example of minimalism. The living room had one couch, two chairs, and a modest flat-screen TV above the mantel. A small table with three seats was located between the living room and what Sydney assumed was the kitchen.

"The restroom is here." T.J. pointed to the door just to his right, but as he locked his gaze with Sydney, he saw she was wide-eyed and almost pale. "What's wrong?"

"This." Sydney held up her hands. "All of this. You sold your beautiful home with what one can describe as a million-dollar view for this. Not only did you give it up, but you did it because of me."

"I'll admit it's a step-down, but it's only a small step."

T.J. walked over to the kitchen table and pulled out the chair. "Please, come sit."

Sydney started to back away. "T.J., I can't. This is too much."

"Please sit and let me explain over dinner." Sydney walked over and sat. T.J. went over to the oven and pulled out a pan. "I've been trying Marty's recipe, but I keep messing up." T.J. looked back at Sydney and explained, "I follow it step by step and still haven't been close to getting it right."

"How many have you made before tonight?" Sydney asked.

"Twenty-two, so here's hoping that lucky number twenty-three is the charm."

T.J. brought over a plate with two slices of pizza and placed it in front of Sydney. She examined it and took a deep breath. "You've nailed the look and the smell."

T.J. took a seat and held up a slice. "After you."

Sydney grabbed a piece and took a bite. She started chewing and began nodding her head. "You did it. There is no difference between this and Marty's pizza, but I have to ask…"

"Go on," T.J. urged. He took a large bite out of his slice.

"Did you make this, or did you get takeout and disguise this as your own?"

T.J. covered his mouth and did the best he could not to laugh. After swallowing, he answered, "That's a fair question, but I did make this."

"Bravo, it is. You've made a pizza equal to that of Marty's."

"Thank you." T.J. took a large bite.

"Didn't you used to work for Marty?" With a cheek full of pizza, T.J. bobbed his head up and down. "Then how come this is your first time making a pizza?"

T.J. held up a finger and hastily chewed his food. With an empty mouth, he said, "Marty kept his dough and sauce ingredients a secret until I bought the business. I was only able to take the dough from the mixer and spread the sauce."

"That makes sense."

"It does, but—" T.J. paused.

"But what?" Sydney asked.

"There was a brief time when I took over for Marty while he was sick. It was just for a few days, but even then, he didn't trust me with the recipe."

Sydney grinned and asked, "You mean there's someone who didn't trust you?"

T.J. chuckled. "That could have been a bad choice of words, but he gave me half and someone else the other half. I was instructed to come at eight a.m. to do my part and then come back at ten when the other person was done."

"Who was the other person?"

T.J. shrugged his shoulders. "Not sure, and I never stayed around to find out."

"You weren't curious?"

"Not really. Marty has always been more than kind and generous to my family, so I respected what he asked and didn't question it."

"Still a funny way of doing things."

"That I cannot argue with, but I owe you answers to everything else." Sydney nodded. "Thanks to Marty you know a lot, so I'm going to start with why here. Why are we at Christmas Town?"

Sydney held her hand in front of her mouth and mumbled, "That's a great start."

"My grandparents built Christmas Town. Except for a few buildings, they built it from the ground up and restored a neglected tree farm to its former glory." Sydney stopped eating and looked at T.J. like a deer staring at headlights. "My mother wasn't ready for a kid, but she knew Uncle Jon, or Jonathan, would do what he always did."

"Bail her out?" Sydney asked.

T.J. nodded. "Part of me thinks she wasn't sure he'd take me, so she named me after him in hopes that it would win him over."

Sydney's voice cracked as she asked, "What about your father?"

"My mom is the only one who knows who he is. She refused to tell and even left his name off the birth certificate."

"Have you ever wondered who he is?"

"When I was little." T.J. leaned back in his chair and scratched his head. "It was hard growing up and seeing others with their dads. I'd see 'em playing catch, fishing, or even eating at Marty's, and it would sting. I know I wasn't the only kid in the world who didn't have a dad, but I felt different. Like, most would know who their dad was or at least know he was a deadbeat, but I didn't have a clue."

Sydney reached across the table. T.J. grabbed her hand as she comforted, "We don't have to talk about this."

"It's fine. You're here for answers and I'm going to give them to you." T.J. cleared his throat. "My grandmother and Jon stepped up and raised me. I look back on it now and I'm grateful to have had them and it's why this place means so much to me." T.J.

smiled and looked around the cabin. "It's also why I have a place to stay."

"I'm sorry. I'm so sorry."

"It's okay." T.J. moved his other hand and covered the rest of Sydney's hand. "Selling the house has allowed me to make things right."

"Make things right?" Sydney's voice rose an octave as she pulled her hands back. "You did nothing wrong to have to make it right. I should be making it right."

"You may have done some things, but I should've been calmer and more level-headed about all of this. Can we just agree that we need a new start and leave all that behind us?"

Without delay, Sydney answered, "Absolutely."

"Good, and continuing with being honest, I'm going to disclose something that no one knows yet."

Sydney held her hand in a stopping gesture and took a long sip of her drink. When she finished, she placed it on the table and explained, "Okay, but if it's big news, break it to me gently. I'm not enjoying all the bombs you're dropping today."

"I'm not sure if this will be easier to swallow, but here it goes. We have one power plant in this region, and up until about a decade ago, maybe two, it supplied power with no problem. Being mostly farmland meant that a small operation would do, but there have been some corporations that have moved in and have started to put a drain on the plant."

"Which is a contributing factor to your solar initiative," Sydney added.

"Yes, but it's still not enough, and your resort is going to put such a strain on the grid that we'll experience either an increase in prices to compensate for the plant's expansion or a rolling blackout."

Sydney leaned back in her chair. "You've cut a deal, haven't you?"

"I have. I've got a meeting tomorrow, but I'm hopeful that it will be a done deal by the end of the day."

"Can I ask what the deal is?"

"In short, your empire will be powered by my solar farm."

"Why tell me? I mean, aren't you worried that I'm going to cut a deal now?"

T.J. leaned back, scratched his head, and without making eye contact, he answered, "Everything about you worries me."

T.J. looked up just enough to see Sydney's smirk. "I'm glad to hear that."

He took a sip of his drink and gently sat it down. "Well, I do have to confess that I've leaked it to the news, so if you undercut me it will forever damage your credibility with the people here."

Sydney laughed, her eyes crinkling. "Well played, but I'll make you a promise if you agree to one thing."

"Go on," T.J. urged.

"I won't go after the power company if you show me around."

T.J. immediately jumped out of his seat and replied, "Deal."

21

Christmas Town

With the sun firmly set, T.J. turned on Christmas Town's lights and led Sydney down the trail to the heart of the village. Along the way, he told Sydney the history of each building until they made it to his favorite spot.

"Here we are," T.J. announced.

Sydney looked around but couldn't see much. There was just a closed shed and a dim glow from the lights behind them. To her, it looked like the end of the road.

"Where are we?" Sydney asked.

"This is my favorite spot." T.J. held up a finger. "Wait one second."

T.J. disappeared around the shed. "You better not be coming back with an axe."

"I won't. It's better...and less violent," he yelled.

"Less?" Sydney asked. "Can it be non-violent?"

The thud of a switch turning and grinding of gears squeaked from the shed. A large rectangular piece of wood broke free from the shed, allowing light to escape. As it rose, T.J. became more visible.

With his head still obstructed from view, T.J. answered, "It all depends on if you're a sore loser."

"Sore loser? What do you mean?" Sydney heard another thud and the night around them turned into day. In front of her was an illuminated mini-golf course. "No way!"

"Yes, way." T.J. was finally in full view, holding a mini-golf putter in each hand. "Chose your putter."

"Or weapon," Sydney whispered.

T.J. squinted his eyes and pulled the putters close. "Did you say weapon?"

"Of course not." Sydney sauntered up to the counter. "It will merely be the instrument of your defeat."

"Perhaps." T.J. looked at the putter in his right hand and looked back at Sydney. "So, which one will it be?"

Sydney looked at each putter and pointed to the one in his left hand. "That one."

"Good choice." T.J. grabbed two red balls and disappeared out of the back of the shed. Quickly appearing from the side, he asked, "Have you played recently?"

"It has been a few years." Sydney looked up and strained her memory. "I was fifteen or sixteen. It was a first and last date."

"First and last?" T.J. handed her a ball.

Sydney walked up to the first hole and placed her ball on the green rubber mat. "He was more concerned with winning than getting to know each other." Sydney took a deep breath and hit the ball. "He'd brag about doing better and pout when he wasn't. It was just a mess."

"Don't do a victory dance. Noted."

The ball glided into the mouth of the polar bear and shot out its right foot. It rolled around toward the hole and stopped just an inch short of falling in.

Sydney looked back at T.J. "I'll try not to."

T.J. placed his ball on the ground, lined up his angle, and tapped the putter against the ball. Instead of going through the bear's mouth, T.J.'s ball went through the bear's left foot. The sound of the ball clanking on steel rang out as the ball ran through the bear, finally appearing out of the tail. The ball slowly made its way down the green until it sank into the hole.

"I'm going to say I got lucky on that one," T.J. informed.

"Hmm, I think we may be looking at ringer here."

"I told you this is my favorite spot."

Hole by hole, Sydney watched T.J. sink each shot with one putt. His ball sneaked past each reindeer leg, cruised around Santa's bag, and dodged every candy cane in Candy Cane Lane. The last hole passed by and ended like all the others—a hole-in-one.

"Okay, how in the world did you do that?"

T.J. shrugged his shoulders and asked, "Did what?"

Sydney started to laugh. "You know what. Eighteen holes and eighteen on the scorecard. How?"

"Follow me," T.J. instructed. They turned and walked back to hole seventeen. "I told you that this was my favorite spot. My grandma and I played this course almost every night when I was a kid. She let me win every time, but I wanted to prove I could win on my own." T.J. stopped midway down the green. "I eventually found all the sweet spots."

"Sweet spots?"

T.J. tapped on the red bumper and waved for Sydney to come over. "You know how pool tables have the dots on the side to allow you to line up shots?"

"Yeah." Sydney looked down and saw a small green dot.

"I did the same with mini-golf. Each dot will allow you to make a hole in one every time."

Sydney started to laugh. "You're an evil genius. Does anyone else know about this?"

T.J. shrugged his shoulders. "Not sure. I've never told anyone, but I'm sure with the number of visitors that we've had throughout the years someone was bound to figure it out."

Sydney turned and surveyed the area. "This is a great place."

"It is." T.J. looked around and smiled.

"So, can I ask you a question?" T.J. waved her on. "How many dates did you bring here and beat this badly?"

"Sally was it. I let her win the first three times we played." T.J. chuckled and rubbed his head. "She called me out on taking it easy on her and demanded a real game. I beat her every game after that for...almost three years."

"Wait. Is she the only girl you dated?"

"Only serious. There have been a few dates here and there, but small-town dating isn't much fun."

"Really? I would have thought it would make it a bit easier. You already know what they like and don't. Makes picking the right person easier."

T.J. shrugged his shoulders. "That does make it easier, but

you miss out on that excitement of getting to know someone." T.J. moved closer to Sydney. "The opportunity to go out and discover the likes and dislikes."

Sydney felt like a teenager once more. She was nervous, anxious, and hopeful. It's what she wished she felt the last time she played mini-golf or on any date since. This was a moment she'd always wanted. A moment where she'd happily lean in for a kiss, one she wished T.J. would take the lead on, but he didn't move. She inched closer, hoping he would get the hint.

"I can see where that would take some of the fun out of things."

T.J. took a step toward Sydney, reached out, and grabbed her hand. He started to lean in and just before it happened, Sydney's phone rang.

"Worst timing ever," Sydney growled.

T.J. pulled back. "You should answer."

"I don't want to."

"The moment will be here when you get back," T.J. insisted.

"I should have left the purse at your place." Sydney reached behind her and pulled her purse around. She looked at the number and groaned. "Be right back." Sydney walked away from T.J. and answered, "I hope this is important."

"I just got off the phone with CC Rides and they had to cancel the contract," Terri informed.

Sydney turned to see how far away T.J. was and if he was looking. They were some distance apart but still in earshot. Through clenched teeth, she asked, "Which contract?"

"All of them."

"Tell me this is a sick joke."

"Wish I could, but it's not. Do you want to game plan?"

"Not really. I was kind of in the middle of something, but I need to start contacting companies." Sydney turned back to T.J. "I'll call you back in an hour."

Sydney hung up and slowly walked back to T.J.

"By the long face, I think it's safe to say the night is over," T.J. inferred.

"Unfortunately, it is. There's been a hiccup with one of the contracts. I need to get back to the room so I can start contacting new builders."

They returned their equipment and drove back to the motel. Sydney didn't get out when the car stopped.

"I—" T.J. started.

"I'm sorry we had to cut it short tonight," Sydney interrupted.

"Me too. It was really nice."

"How about a rain check?" Sydney asked.

"I've got a busy day tomorrow, but I think we could have dinner if that's okay."

"I'd like that, but no pressure if you can't work it out. I'm not going anywhere."

"Me either."

Sydney got out of the car truck and went into her room.

2 2

Rain Check

Sydney opened the door and started to step outside. T.J. was standing on his tiptoes trying to peer into the room.

"Anxious to see my room?" Sydney grinned.

"Well, you know we had a deal. I share my secrets and you show me your plans."

"You owe me dinner first."

"I thought this was going to be your treat?"

Sydney jogged over to the truck and yelled, "Nope."

T.J. hopped in and started the engine. "Good thing I planned for this."

They drove back to Christmas Town but not to the cabin. T.J. took them down a worn-out dirt path and stopped just a few feet from the top of a hill. They got out and walked to the top.

"This is it," T.J. informed.

Sydney looked around at the clear view of the surroundings.

She could see Christmas Town, farmland, and patches of wood for what appeared to be miles.

"This is stunning."

"It was my grandmother's favorite spot to come and unwind. When she went up here alone, we knew to leave her alone."

"I can see why she liked it. You can see—"

"Everything." Sydney felt a hand on her hip and T.J.'s arm reaching over the top of her shoulder. He pointed straight ahead. "Depending on how you build, your resort will be right there."

"Do you think your grandmother would approve of the view change?"

"I think we're past the point of trying to figure out likes and don't likes. I think she would just make the best of what it became."

T.J. disappeared but Sydney kept looking out at the scenery. She heard the truck door open and then close. Out of the corner of her eye, she saw T.J. lying down a blanket. She turned to see a cooler resting beside the blanket.

"Looks like I'm in for a treat."

"Come have a seat." Sydney sat down, T.J. moved the cooler over, and sat across from Sydney. "I figured you've eaten at every restaurant we have so I thought I'd make you something special."

T.J. opened the cooler and the smell of hickory smoke meat spewed from the confines.

Sydney took a deep breath. "That smells wonderful."

T.J. pulled out plates, silverware, and napkins. He then passed over a can of soda and a bottle of water.

"I didn't know which one you would want."

"They're both fine." Next T.J. pulled out two foiled-wrapped items and passed one to Sydney. "I hope this tastes as good as it smells."

"Hopefully, it will."

Sydney peeled back the foil to expose a slice of bread. She peeled the slice up gently to expose a mixture of peanut butter and jelly.

She started to laugh. "This was—clever." She looked over at T.J. "How did you get the smell?"

T.J. pulled out a large ball of foil and revealed wood chips. "I warmed these up and closed the lid. Instant illusion."

Sydney took a bite. After swallowing, she said, "You make the finest PB&J I've ever had."

T.J. held his up and replied, "Thank you."

With her hand over her mouth, she asked, "Why did you pick here?"

T.J. shrugged his shoulders. "I don't know really. It just seemed right because of what we're going through. We both could use a calming place."

"This certainly is the spot. So, what would be a good way I can get to know you better?"

"I'll answer any question as long as it's not business-related and you must do the same."

For the next hour, they did a fifty-question style of getting to know each other. With each passing question, they moved closer to each other and as the sun began to fade they went from sitting to lying down. They continued to talk while looking at the emerging stars. Just as Sydney felt like she could spend the night there, she felt a tap on her shoulder.

"Come on. I need to get you back before it's too late."

"Afraid I'll turn into a pumpkin?" Sydney locked eyes with T.J.

Finally, he cleared his throat and said, "I believe you owe me a look at—"

"The Ridge," Sydney finished.

"Really? The Ridge?"

"What's wrong with that? I thought it would be fitting."

"Nothing wrong. I just didn't think you dug that deep into the history here."

"To be fair it wasn't that deep. The county website explained the moving of millions of tons of dirt to level the land in the first two sentences," Sydney explained.

T.J. sat up and asked, "How about we go take a look at the plans for The Ridge?"

The peace Sydney felt moments ago was replaced with dread.

23

The Ridge

T.J. put the truck in park. "So, how does it feel?"

"Not good at all," Sydney answered.

"Really? Last night here and you're not good?"

"Oh, that."

"Yes, that. What did you think I meant?"

Sydney shook her head. "Nothing."

Sydney opened the door and got out of the truck. She wasted no time getting into the room. She flipped on the lights and scurried around, but to no end—the table was full of drawings, the project board with much of the same, and files were scattered all over her bed. Sydney didn't know what to hide, what to show, or what to do. She felt sick to her stomach and the knock at the door made it worse.

"Can I come in?" T.J. asked.

"Uh, yeah. Sure." The door opened fully, and T.J. walked in.

"I just... I don't—" T.J. walked straight to the projected board. She watched as he examined each image. "I don't know what to say."

"You're going to have mini-golf." He turned to Sydney and pointed at the board. "Indoor and outdoor."

"Yes, but—"

"Go-carts too." He turned back to the board. "Ice skating."

"Let me explain," Sydney pleaded.

"You've got everything that Christmas Town has but it's all bigger." T.J. looked at Sydney with sheer terror. He looked as though he saw a ghost or was looking at Death. "I knew we'd have some of the same things." T.J. snapped his head back to the board. "No matter what I do —what we do— Christmas Town can't compete with this."

"You don't have to compete. Christmas Town is beautiful. People—"

"You're going to have all that we offer." T.J. walked over to the table and looked through the pictures. "Plus a golf course, driving range, theme park, restaurants, and the list goes on. Only part of your plan was released."

"T.J., just listen."

He threw up his hands. "Go on."

Sydney opened her mouth, but nothing came out. She stepped toward T.J. and explained, "I didn't think it would be like this."

"Like what?" T.J. waved his left hand around the table and his other at the project board. "You knew what you were doing from the start. This proves without a doubt that you were going run us out."

"I knew but I didn't expect this." She repeatedly pointed between herself and T.J.

"I got to go."

"T.J. please don't leave. Not like this. Let's talk."

"I've got—"

T.J. didn't finish his sentence. Lost for words, he walked out the door.

24

Family Meeting: Part III

T.J. walked into his cabin, and he wasn't alone. Beth and Jonathan sat at the kitchen table.

As soon as they saw T.J., Beth opened her mouth. "I think you have some explaining to do."

T.J. walked to the refrigerator and grabbed a soda. He cracked it open and leaned against the counter. "Where do you want me to start?"

"I think with why you are staying here?"

"I sold the house and needed a place to stay."

"You did what?" Beth screeched.

"Please say you're joking," Jonathan pleaded.

"The short story is that I needed the money to pay off all my debt and the rest is going into paying down what Christmas Town owes."

"You shouldn't have done that. We're going to make it."

Jonathan remained calm but T.J. knew that behind that comforting voice, a storm was building.

"I'm not so sure. I've gotten to know Sydney well—"

"What? Why?" Beth asked with a pitch that would make dogs cover their ears.

"In short, she's great to be around, but also I've wanted to learn more about her intention and I just found out what she intends to do."

"Well don't hold back. Tell us," Beth demanded.

"Santa's Workshop is the only thing we'll have over her resort. They're going to have mini-golf, go-carts, ice skating, and all of it is bigger and better than what we have. Between that and all the other things that we don't offer, they'll be able to keep people so entertained and well-fed that they won't need to venture off property."

"What if we upgrade?" Beth asked.

Not allowing T.J. to answer Jonathan asked, "So I take it that you've seen her plans?"

"I have. We could upgrade, but the problem is money. It's hard to say how much an expansion would cost and we don't know if it would pay off."

"Are we just going to give up?" Beth asked.

"No. Mom wouldn't do that, and neither are we," Jonathan replied.

"I've got a plan that may keep us afloat," T.J. said.

Beth threw up her hands. "And you're waiting for what?"

"I bought Mr. White's land and talked with Stuart at the power plant to make a solar farm. I'm not an expert in the whole conversion rates and all that—"

"You're going to power the resort!" Beth yelled.

"Jesus, Beth. Calm down," Jonathan ordered. "We need a level head here."

T.J. defended himself. "If I don't jump on this, then Stuart will go to someone else, and we need to think bigger than a remodel. Once the check from my house clears, White's land will be paid for and all the income from the solar farm will be profit."

"What about equipment?" Jonathan asked.

"The plant needs a solar farm more than we do, so Stuart is going to supply all the equipment. The only problem is the profit will be minimal until the equipment is paid for."

Beth was about to speak but Jonathan raised his hand for her to stop. "Let's say all your plans work. What does that mean for Christmas Town?"

"I think it will lead to what we've already talked about. We'd have to close parts down and the workers may become family only."

Beth began rubbing her hands through her hair. The frustration was visible. With her head down, she asked, "Jonathan, what did Dave say about the finances?"

"Same thing that T.J.'s saying. The only difference will be what T.J. adds with his house sale and the solar farm. We can refinance the loan and make the most of the years until the resort is built." Jonathan pointed to T.J. "That farm is what's going to save us from closing all the doors."

Beth stood up and started walking away. "Aunt Beth, where are you going?"

"I need some time alone to think."

The front door closed as quickly as it opened, and it was just Jonathan and T.J. standing in the kitchen.

"I tried Uncle Jon. I really tried."

"I know and you did too much."

"I thought she was here to run Christmas Town out, so I thought buying the land beside what they purchased would have made her look elsewhere."

"A little naive to think you would have done that with just one lot of land, don't you think?"

"A bit, but Mrs. Jefferson isn't selling out."

"So that's why they haven't bought in Carrell."

"No point in trying to cut us off if you can't get all the land."

Jonathan released a laugh. "Isn't that something?"

"What?" T.J. asked.

"Your plan worked. You kept them from building here."

T.J. started to laugh, but stopped and scratched his head. "Yeah, I guess I did. I thought I could get some land in Henry, but Sydney has deeper pockets than mine."

"Speaking of Sydney, how was your date last night?" Jonathan grinned while T.J. stared with wide eyes. "Come on. You didn't think I wouldn't notice the lights turn on? The lights, mind you, are off because it's our repair and cleaning week. Then you're gone again almost all day and night."

T.J. smiled and shook his head. "Last night was nice and tonight was great. Well, great until I saw her plans."

"So, you like her then?"

"I do but—"

"But you think that pursuing anything with her would cause a family rift." T.J. nodded. "Want to know what your grandma would say?"

T.J. laughed. "I can imagine a hundred different scenarios, so I might as well hear what you think."

"Sydney may or may not be your one, but you'll never know for sure if you don't find out."

T.J. laughed, and between his breaths, he asked, "Is that before or after she kicked my butt out the door?"

"You know as well as I do that you'd get the kick before she said it and after."

T.J. raised his drink and replied, "True." He took a sip and rinsed out the can in the sink. "What do you think?

"I think you have given such much to Christmas Town and Fenton that you owe it to yourself to think about you for once." Jonathan cleared his throat. "I'm not trying to pry into personal matters but how did the night end?"

"I saw her plans and she didn't have an explanation, so I rushed out and came straight here."

"You should give her a call." Jonathan patted T.J. on the shoulder. "Sooner rather than later.

Before Jonathan could walk out the door, T.J. asked, "Is it okay if I'm a long-term resident?"

"Christmas Town is our home. It's not mine or your aunt's, but *ours*."

"Thanks."

Jonathan nodded and walked out.

T.J. walked over to the couch, took a seat, and pulled out his phone. He pulled up his messages, found Sydney's chain, and started to type. In the end, T.J. hit delete and erased the message. He did this a dozen times, and each time he saw the message bubble pop up. Sydney was doing the same, but T.J. never got a message, nor did he end up sending one.

25

Marty

"For the love that is all that is holy and unholy, hit send," Marty shouted.

T.J.'s hands froze and his head jerked up. "What?"

"Hit send."

"I wasn't—I was looking for something. I wasn't texting." T.J. winced. He wasn't even convinced.

"You're typing away and then hitting delete." Marty started to walk around the counter. "Type, type, type, and then delete, delete, delete. You've done it so much that I swear you're going to wear that part of the screen out." Marty took a seat across from T.J. and huffed, "Why do you kids think anyone my age knows nothing about technology? If anything, you need to give my generation more credit because we've used more types of technology than you."

T.J. sat his phone on the table. "Fine."

"Fine? That's not an apology."

"I'm sorry. You're right."

"Of course I'm right. Now, tell me why you won't hit send?"

"Because I don't know what to say."

"Telling her how you feel is a great start."

T.J. looked up at Marty, eyes glossy. "I don't think Christmas Town is going to survive and it's going to close because of the woman I want to date. How—how can I be with someone who is the reason for that? Every time I see her I'm going to see the person who destroyed Grandma's legacy."

Marty nodded. "You're not going to want to hear this, but her legacy isn't Christmas Town. It's you. Now, I love your aunt and uncle but they don't have what you have and you have what your grandmother had."

"I'm not sure I follow."

"Their priority during all this was to save Christmas Town. I mean, sure, I understand. Christmas Town is their livelihood, but your first thought was the community."

"Well, as much I wish to say that was true, I was thinking about Christmas Town too."

Marty quickly raised his finger and pointed. "Right there. You added too. Even if the thought was simultaneous, you wanted to take care of the people here. You're taking care of this community the same way Sara used to and that's her legacy."

T.J. leaned back and gently rested his head on the wall. "It makes sense, but I just need time to come to terms with it."

"T.J., you need to come to terms with the fact that Christmas Town hasn't closed. You're letting something that hasn't happened and may not happen ruin your shot at a future."

Marty stood up and ordered, "Now, I must ask you to leave. Your moping is making me sad and I don't want to be sad."

Marty began shooing his hands until T.J. left. He went back to the kitchen and prepared two calzones. Ten minutes later the door chimed and Marty shouted,

"Take a seat and I'll be out in just a minute."

He grabbed the ladle, dipped it in the sauce, and poured it into the plastic containers. He placed them on the serving tray with the two calzones and brought them out to his awaiting patron.

"How did you know it was me?" Sydney asked.

"Every day for a bit now you've been coming in here between 1:15 and 1:30, which is roughly fifteen to thirty minutes after T.J. leaves." He placed a calzone in front of Sydney and one across from her. "Drink?"

"Pepsi, please." Marty rushed behind the counter and filled two cups with ice. As he poured Sydney asked, "Is it that obvious?"

"That you two are avoiding each other?" Marty laughed. "I was trying to think of something witty, but I'll be straightforward. Of course it is."

"Has he asked about me?"

"Not with words." Marty returned with the drink.

"How else would he ask?"

"All I'm going to say is that you're both being stubborn about it all. Both moping about—."

"He's been moping?"

"You say that like you haven't. You have to either tell me what's wrong or you're going to have to stop coming here."

Sydney looked up at Marty. "Do you want to lose my business?"

"No. You're a great tipper. All kidding aside, you two need to talk. Pick up the phone and give him a call. You need to talk."

"I've tried." Marty started eating and gave Sydney a hard stare. "Okay, I haven't said anything. I've started a thousand messages but ended up deleting them."

"Why aren't you sending?"

"I'm worried about how all this is going to pan out. What if Christmas Town closes? How would our relationship be after that?" Sydney cleared her throat. "Our business and personal relationship."

"If Christmas Town goes under, will you still be in business?"

"Of course," Sydney answered.

"If it stays open, will you still be in business?"

Reluctantly, Sydney answered, "Yes."

"You need to come to terms with that no matter what happens, you, T.J., and I are all in this together. We're going to see each other driving down the road, crossing the street, eating out, or getting groceries. The only difference with me is that it won't be awkward when I see either of you, but you two will have the next fifty-plus years together. Those years will pass a lot easier if you make amends."

Sydney nodded. "You're right."

"Of course I am. I'm always right."

***

Sydney took a bite and looked at Marty as he chewed.

He had just finished one conversation but his eyes were telling another. He was avoiding eye contact as best as possible, but it just took a glimpse to see his pain. Sydney had heard much of Marty's story, but those watery eyes were screaming at her.

"So Marty, I hate to pry but what are you not telling me?"

Slowly, Marty looked up. He took a deep breath and explained, "Thirty years ago, about six percent of kids left after high school. Twenty years ago, it was about nineteen percent, and ten years ago it was forty-five. Last year seventy percent of the graduating class left for either college, trade school, or just left."

"I didn't realize that."

Marty nodded. "I want the kids of this community to better themselves, but I also want this community to be around a century after I'm gone. The resort can help with keeping them here."

"Exactly! That's what I want too."

"But," Marty held up a finger, "I'm worried about this place."

"Oh."

"I got sick a few years ago and was forced to close. I wasn't even in the hospital for a day when T.J. opened the doors."

Sydney smiled. "Why am I not surprised? He's one-of-a-kind."

"He is, and he kept the business going for me, but also found my books. I was barely making a profit and there was no way that I was going to be able to afford the medical bills, so he made an offer." Marty got up from the table and walked behind the counter. He started to rub his hands across the wood.

"You made the deal to pay your medical bills."

Marty nodded. "Most would say that he was taking advantage of me, but he wasn't. No one else would've been able to buy this place, and if they had, then they wouldn't have allowed me to stay. He helped me at my lowest by allowing me to choose when I leave."

"Are you okay? Health-wise?"

"No, and to be honest, the odds are that I won't make it to see your resort open." Marty grinned as Sydney walked to the counter. "Then again, I may be too stubborn to pass."

"Can I help? I know some great doctors, and don't worry about the cost."

Marty reached across the counter and grabbed her by the hand. "You're too sweet, but I need you to do one thing for me instead."

"Anything."

"Make things right with T.J. and Christmas Town. Show him that both can survive, and both will breathe new life into this community."

"I don't know how."

"You may not at this moment, but you'll figure it out." Sydney nodded. "Oh, and one more thing."

"Of course."

"Make sure this place never closes," Marty pleaded.

Sydney looked up, down, and side to side. She smiled and said, "I think I may have an idea that will keep the doors open."

26

Parley: Part III

"Hello," Beth answered.

"Hello, I'd like to speak to the owners of Christmas Town," the voice said.

"This is Beth. I'm one of them."

"Oh good. This is the third transfer. I'm Juan Garcia of Garcia Entertainment."

Beth frantically waved her arms at Jonathan and T.J. She placed the phone on speaker. "Mr. Garcia, I have two of the other owners here with me."

"Hello, Mr. Garcia. I'm Jonathan Cunningham."

"T.J. Cunningham, sir."

"Ah, T.J. I've heard a lot of good things about you," Juan said.

Before T.J. could respond, Beth asked, "What can we do for you, Mr. Garcia?"

"I'm in town and would like to discuss some business."

Beth hit mute. "Absolutely not."

"We have to hear him out," Jonathan retorted.

They both looked at T.J. He shrugged his shoulders and asked, "What?"

"No, right?" Beth's eyes were wide and pleading.

"We need to hear what he has to say," Jonathan insisted.

Beth leaned against the table, as if T.J. wouldn't be able to hear otherwise. "Do you know what it's about, T.J.? Has Sydney said anything?"

"We haven't spoken in weeks," T.J. informed.

Beth pinched her eyes closed as she leaned back. "What? I thought you two were a thing."

Quickly changing the topic, T.J. urged, "Let's hear him out."

"Fine, but we're coming back to you and Sydney thing," Beth said. She hit the button again. "When would you like to meet?"

"The sooner the better. I'm at Sydney's house."

"We can be there within the hour," Jonathan said.

"Excellent. See you soon."

Beth rushed out of the room, and Jonathan looked over his shoulder to make sure she was gone.

He waltzed over to T.J., leaned in, and whispered, "What happened between you and Sydney?"

"I blew it," T.J. admitted.

"What did you do?"

"It's what I didn't do." T.J. looked at his uncle who was as wide-eyed as Beth had been. "I didn't do anything. I never called or texted."

"Why?"

"I tried. I started to type, but then stopped. I'd start back up and then stop again. I must have done it a hundred times. I just didn't know what to say."

"I suggest you start finding the words because you're going to get your chance to talk soon enough."

T.J. practiced what he'd say to Sydney the entire way to his former home. He'd say a line, repeat it, and then come up with something new. By the time he got to the door, he hadn't settled on anything. Before he could knock, the door opened and the person standing before him wasn't Sydney. The man was close to the same height, had a stocky build, and had a salt-and-pepper beard that matched his hair.

"Welcome," he announced. "Please come in." He moved back from the doorway and T.J. entered. Jonathan and Beth followed close behind. "I'm Juan Garcia and it is a pleasure to meet you all."

"Jonathan."

Juan extended his hand. "Nice to meet you, Jonathan."

Jonathan embraced the hand and replied, "And you, also."

Instead of shaking hands, Beth waved her limb and proclaimed, "I'm Beth."

"A pleasure." Juan turned toward T.J. "Which makes you T.J."

"Yes, sir." T.J. held out his hand, but Juan didn't embrace it. Instead, he hugged T.J.

"I owe you a huge debt," Juan whispered.

Once released, T.J. said, "I don't understand."

"Come in." Juan led them to the kitchen where they sat around the table. "This project was given to Sydney as a reward for years of hard work."

"Couldn't be too many years as young as she is," Beth snapped.

T.J. jerked his head to Beth. He mouthed, "Stop," and turned back to Juan. "Forgive my aunt."

Juan chuckled. "It's fine. She's been an official employee since she was fifteen. It started with secretary-like duties, but I began teaching her how to run things. She's secured some of the best-selling artists the company has ever signed. Sydney also bought the rights to my fourth highest-grossing movie. She has a crazy eye for talent in all forms."

"I understand the intentions, but why here?" Jonathan asked.

"We scouted many areas, but ultimately chose here due to the availability of land and the potential of the town. There are many closed and run-down spaces that will make for a great opportunity."

"Not to interrupt the flow of the story again, but I'm still confused about you owing me a debt."

"Ah, yes. Well, though this was a reward for Sydney, I wanted to see how she would handle things with the community. Our resort will be successful no matter what, but what will it do to this community?" He held up a finger. "What will it do to Christmas Town?"

"Put us out of business. That's what," Beth mumbled.

T.J. slammed his hand on the table. "That's enough, Aunt Beth!" Beth looked at T.J. in sheer terror. No one—even his family—had ever seen T.J. angry or raise his voice. "All of this is hard enough. It affects more than just you, so knock it off."

Beth looked at the ceiling, avoiding eye contact with T.J. Taking a deep breath, she said, "You're right. I'm sorry."

"Continue Mr. Garcia," T.J. encouraged.

"When Sydney came here, she was set on doing whatever it takes and didn't care what happened to the businesses around here. It was through T.J. that she realized the importance of caring about the community."

"Oh." T.J. sat back in his chair and scratched his head. "I wish—"

"She's been having the same regrets," Juan assured. "And that's why we're here today. I want to offer you a non-compete contract." Juan handed out a small packet of paper to each of them. "I'm going to go outside so that you all can discuss."

T.J. waited for Juan to leave to begin reading. He flipped the pages, turned back to the front, and read the contract again. After his second pass through the contract, he placed it on the table and leaned back in the chair once more.

"No one is going to say anything?" Beth asked. "We can't accept this."

"I don't want to," Jonathan replied.

"We have to," T.J. added.

"What!" Beth shot up from her chair and started to walk away, but she quickly turned around, not able to resist voicing her opinion. "If we give up attractions now, where will it end?"

"Their way leads to Christmas Town staying open. Your way leads to Christmas Town closing," T.J. informed.

"You don't know that," Beth insisted.

"I do. Dave ran the numbers. Uncle Jon ran the numbers. I've run the numbers, and I'm telling you that in ten years we will be on life support or a ghost town. The only people who will stay at Christmas Town will be those who can't afford to stay at the resort but will have enough money to spend at the theme park."

"He's right, Beth. We're going to have to close some things anyway."

"Yes, but not the mini-golf, skating rinks, or the go-carts. They're our money-makers, Jonathan."

"And he's offering more money than they're worth. Not to mention he wants to help build a wedding venue."

"A venue that would be exclusive to us alone," T.J. added.

"I just don't like it." Beth shook her head and walked away.

"Go with her and I'll talk with Mr. Garcia." T.J. didn't wait for a response and walked out to the deck. "Mr. Garcia."

"Ah, T.J. Come." Juan gazed out to the tree line. "This is a magnificent spot."

"It is indeed."

"There's only one problem with it."

T.J. chuckled. "I'm curious."

Juan turned to T.J. "I don't like how we got it." Juan motioned for T.J. to take a seat. "I truly believe that a person's home is their castle. It's their retreat from the stress of life, and this is not just any castle. No, you built this castle for yourself. You designed all of it, and no one told you what you could or couldn't have."

T.J. nodded. "It's true."

"That is why I don't like how we got this, but how we got this is why I agreed to make that proposal."

"Agree to it? This wasn't your idea?"

"No, this was all Sydney." Juan started to rub his chin and asked, "What do you think of this deal?"

"It's a blessing and a curse." T.J. leaned forward. "When your resort is fully operational...the impact could be devastating. You're bigger and better and will certainly take business from us. It's business that could cause us to close, so this deal would save us, but—"

"Go on," Juan urged.

"But Christmas Town isn't just an attraction. It's a place where people have grown up. A place where families have made memories and started traditions. It's the place of first dates." T.J. shook his head. "I know it's silly to even hesitate at your offer, but—"

"Hesitating for something that means so much to you isn't silly. I know this offer isn't easy, and to be honest, it wasn't exactly easy for me either. I'm offering millions for just a few things that will cost me nothing to put you out of business, but I'm offering it because I want us to work together. In fifty years, I want The Ridge and Christmas Town to be standing side by side and flourishing. I want my great-grandchildren to walk into Christmas Town's bakery and get a world-renowned cookie fresh from the oven. I want them to sit on Santa's lap and lie about how good they've been."

T.J. laughed. "That sounds nice, and honestly I think we can make it happen. My aunt is on the fence, and we still have to discuss it a bit more."

Juan stood and held out his hand. "How about three days? Does seventy-two hours to give me your final answer sound fair?"

T.J. rose and shook hands. "That's fair." T.J. started for the door but stopped before reaching for the knob. "Mr. Garcia, would you be willing to tell me where I can find Sydney?"

"She's at the construction site. I'll let security know you're coming."

"Thank you."

T.J. drove his aunt and uncle back to Christmas Town and left without saying where he was going or when he'd be back. He simply put the truck in reverse and drove off to The Ridge.

27

Welcome to The Ridge

"Mr. Cunningham, I presume." T.J. hadn't come to a complete stop or had time to respond when the guard directed, "Keep straight until you see the trailers. Park beside the trucks and trailers on the right, and Ms. Garcia's office is the lone trailer on the other side of the road."

"Thank you."

T.J. drove down the dirt road and the signs of progress were all around: acres of trees had been cleared and loggers were busy clearing even more, miles of piping were stacked higher than T.J.'s truck and giant spools of wires seemed almost endless. Half a mile in, trailers were nestled just off the side of the road. There were five trailers on the right with a row of trucks parked in front. He pulled up beside the last one, got out of his truck, and took a long stare at the lone trailer across the road.

As he walked toward the scene, he noticed the blinds on a

window had a slight opening. Though the face couldn't be seen, the hast at which the crack shut let T.J. know that it was Sydney watching. He smiled, shook his head, and continued to the trailer. The short walk was filled with the rehearsal of what he was going to say and how he was going to explain his silence. As he stood at the door trying to decide if he should make a run for it or knock, the door opened.

"Hey," T.J. said.

"Hey." Sydney opened the door fully, took a step back, and waved him in. "Come in."

"Thanks."

T.J. walked in and looked around. It was like the waiting room of a doctor's office. There were single chairs on both sides of the room, a water cooler, and a coffee table with magazines. The door to the far side of the trailer was labeled "Rest Room."

T.J. turned back to Sydney. "I hope you don't mind me just stopping by, but I met with your father this morning—"

"No, it's fine, but let's go into my office." Sydney was standing just a couple of feet in front of her office door, and she quickly led the way, walking inside. When T.J. entered, she closed the door and offered, "Would you like to have a seat?"

"Sure, thanks." T.J. took a seat but Sydney didn't go behind her desk. Instead, she sat beside him. Looking into her eyes he said, "I'm sorry for the way I handled things."

"Me too." Sydney pointed to herself. "I mean, I'm sorry for the way I handled things also."

"I tried to message. I started to—"

"I know. I saw the bubbles pop up hundreds of times."

T.J. winced. "I didn't think you saw that."

Sydney laughed. "How did you not see me typing? I tried to reach out, but I didn't know what to say."

"Me either. I was—"

"Hurt?"

"Yeah, but for many reasons. When I saw your plans, I freaked out because they're incredible. If you compare our mini-golf courses alone, Christmas Town is a Model T and The Ridge is the U.S.S. Enterprise."

Sydney was holding back a giggle. "It's not that bad."

"It's true. We've taken care of Christmas Town, but we're dated. What you're going to offer is better, and I'm not upset about that." Sydney tilted her head and squinted. "Okay, I'm a bit upset, but there's nothing I can do about it. We can't afford to upgrade, and even if we did, you have the funds to go even bigger."

"That's true."

"Which is why I want to take you up on your offer."

"Is there a but coming?"

"No. I think we should take it. Your offer is more than generous, and it will solve all our problems."

"Still sounds like there's a but coming."

T.J. scratched his head. "It's not a *but* in the traditional sense, but my aunt is a bit of a hard sell."

"She hates the proposal?"

"With a passion, but I'm certain I can get her to sign."

"Got any ideas as to how you're going to do that?"

"I'm going to prepare a presentation with four slides. The first has a picture of Christmas Town as it currently stands. The next three will be pictures of Christmas Town in twenty, forty, and sixty years. Each picture after the first shows the dilapidation of Christmas Town with each picture getting worse and worse until the last shows a decrepit ghost town."

"That's a bold plan."

"It's somewhat of a joke, but I may do it."

"How long do you have to decide?"

"Three days, but I'm going to see if we can sign tonight."

"That would be great." Sydney got up and walked behind her desk. She opened a drawer and retrieved a folder. "I had a feeling I'd see you after you met with Dad, so I saved this for when you got here."

Sydney handed over the folder and T.J. opened it, starting to read the contents. When finished, he closed the folder and placed it on his lap.

"I don't understand."

"I know it has some big words, but it's pretty straightforward."

"No." T.J. laughed. "I mean, what is this? Why?"

"You know how theme parks will have a specialty food vendor?" T.J. nodded. "I want Marty's to be that vendor. We'll have three or four stands where you can get pizza by the slice and a full-scale restaurant in the resort."

"Why would you do this? Your offer for Christmas Town is generous enough. Beyond generous, really."

"I've become a regular a Marty's and we talked. He told me what you did for him, and he made me make him a promise."

"Oh, you didn't. You know he's as tricky as Rumpelstiltskin, right?"

Sydney laughed at the thought. "He kind of is, isn't he?"

T.J nodded. "He said business hasn't been doing that well and made me promise that there will always be a Marty's."

T.J. held up the folder. "That would surely do it, but there are many things to consider."

"Like what?"

"If there is a full restaurant at the park with slice stands throughout, what will happen to the original building? Will there be any dues? Will we get enough guests to keep the original building running?"

"That's a good point that I didn't think about, but these are some things we can work out later."

"Like?" T.J. asked.

"We could make the park restaurant resort exclusive, have a different but Marty-approved menu, or hand out coupons exclusive to the original building. There won't be any dues. We will take on all the building expenses and upkeep, but you can cover the salary for the employees."

"Those are some great ideas." T.J. opened the folder. "One last question."

"I'm all ears."

"Why did you do all this for us? I mean, be honest—why did you come up with this?"

"I've seen all you do and what you've done for the community, and I want to be like that. I don't want us to be seen as a destroyer of communities or a breaker of traditions—I want us to be united and build this community up."

"That does sound better than a feud that leaves me homeless. Well, more homeless than I already am."

"It does, and to be honest that is only part of the reason."

Sydney bounced her head back and forth. "A major part, but still just a part."

"What's the other minor part that's just as important but not as big of a deal?"

Sydney blushed and refused to meet T.J.'s eyes as she said, "You. It's because of you. I thought we had a connection before I blew it."

Sydney didn't look at T.J. until the final word was out of her mouth, and when she looked up, his gaze latched onto her with gratefulness. "I thought so too," he replied. "I mean not that you blew it, but the connection piece."

Sydney smiled. "I knew what you meant."

T.J. placed the folder on the desk and asked, "Should I go ahead and sign now?"

"You can but I want you to know that this offer is going to stand if Christmas Town doesn't sign the non-compete."

"I appreciate that." T.J. grabbed the closet pen and signed his name.

"So, what now?"

"Would you mind coming to my cabin tonight around eight?"

"Depends on why I'm coming over. Is it as a friend, business partner, or something else?"

T.J. stood up and started for the door. "Let's call it friends that are looking for something else," he said over his shoulder.

Sydney got up and moved to her desk chair. "In that case, I will see you tonight."

"See you tonight."

28

Family Meeting: Part IV

"Where have you been?" Beth yelled. She was standing as straight as a Christmas tree and her face glowed brighter than its lights. In a comic book, the glare from her eyes would've resulted in laser beams coming out.

"Would you please relax?" T.J. asked.

"How can I? You were there. You know what they want us to give up."

Uncle Jonathan sighed. "You're lucky, T.J. I've been dealing with this since you left. Speaking of which, where did you go? Why didn't you say anything? You just drove off without saying a word."

"I went to talk to Sydney," T.J. answered.

Aunt Beth gawked. "Tell me you turned her down."

"I wish I could say I wasn't curious, but I'm intrigued," Jonathan said.

T.J. headed to the conference table and took a seat. Jonathan and Beth followed. T.J. cleared his throat. "She offered a business contract with Marty's that will save it from going under."

"Offered? You didn't sign?" Jonathan asked.

"I did," T.J. answered.

Beth placed her elbows on the table, cupped her hands together, and placed them on her forehead. "Please say you're joking," Beth pleaded.

"Aunt Beth, I love you, but you're being as stubborn as a mule. You've seen the numbers, you know the problem, and yet you refuse to recognize the simple fact that if we don't co-exist with The Ridge, Christmas Town won't exist at all."

"That's not true," Beth insisted.

Uncle Jonathan spoke up. "It is, and you need to come to terms with that. Besides, T.J. and I are the major holders of the company and don't need your signature. Mom had it written that decisions don't need to be unanimous, just the majority. We're the majority, but we'd like it if you were okay with the decision."

"Or you could buy me out," T.J. suggested.

Beth stood with eyes as wide as saucers. "Why—why would you say that? I've—"

"You've what? Poured your heart and soul into Christmas Town? Worked until you got blisters? What do you think we did? I grew up here just as much if not more than you. You left to go to school, got married, had a family, and started a life before you came back. But I was here."

"T.J.—" Beth pleaded.

"I was *here*!" T.J. scorned. "You're not the only one who

cares about this place. This place means more to me than anyone in the family, and without Christmas Town, without Grandma, I have nothing." T.J. stood up. "I'm done talking about this."

T.J. was almost at the door when Jonathan urged, "T.J., come back so we can properly discuss this."

He stopped and turned back to his uncle. "If you don't sign, then you need to find the money to buy me out. I refuse to be the one who closes Christmas Town."

T.J. opened the door and walked out.

29

What now?

"Can you believe that?" Beth turned to Jonathan.

Jonathan nodded his head, almost violently. "Absolutely."

"What?" Beth snapped. "You can't be on his side."

"Why is this so hard for you to accept? We keep repeating the same things over and over and you won't face the reality we're up against."

Tears started to form in her eyes. "It's because you're so quick to give up what Mom and Dad built. They want us to gut the heart of Christmas Town."

"The fact that you see the heart of Christmas Town as just a few rides shows how little you know about this place." Jonathan stood up, walked over to the window, and looked out. "Relationships are what this place is built on. Every year, the community came out in droves to support Mom and Dad."

"And they've been doing the same for us," Beth reminded.

"Yes, but it's their word of mouth that brought the visitors."

"And they'll keep coming."

"Will they? Would you?" Jonathan asked.

"Would I what?"

"Would you come here instead of The Ridge? Would your kids rather ride a half-mile track or a two-mile track that goes under bridges and has a tunnel? Would they want to risk mini-golf in the cold instead of playing in one of the two indoor greens?"

"Here of course," Beth answered.

"Beth, take a step back and think about it. A rustic cabin experience where you cook all your food or go to the local restaurants versus an upscale cabin, five-start resort, with gourmet cooking at your fingertips... Christmas Town doesn't stand a chance. The Ridge has roller coasters, games, ice skating, a water park, and more. Where would you go?" Beth stood quietly and avoided eye contact. Jonathan stared at Beth and repeated, "Where would you go?"

"The Ridge," Beth mumbled.

"And that's why we need to form a relationship with them. That contract ensures we keep the doors open."

"Sure this contract does, but what about the next? We give in now and they're going to do it again and again. It won't end until they completely buy us out."

"That won't happen."

"How do you know? How can you guarantee that?"

Jonathan walked over to the contract and shook it violently. "This gives us the money to pay all our debt, build a wedding venue, and have enough money left over to start a trust fund whose interest pays for our upkeep alone. Why would we sell out if all our needs are met?"

"I don't know." Beth turned to Jonathan with tears flowing. "I just don't want to see it go. I don't want to see—"

"Beth, do you realize what happened a few moments ago? T.J. is willing to have us buy him out. T.J. of all people is wanting out."

"He's—"

"You weren't here, Beth."

She shook her head. "What do you mean?"

"When Mom asked to put him on the payroll he was five." Jonathan took a seat. "He woke up an hour before her to cook them breakfast." Beth sat next to him, hanging on to his words. "Mom found him dressed and ready to go while eating waffles fresh from the toaster. He told her to eat up, and when she asked what he was doing he answered, 'Going to work.' T.J. helped her bake all the cookies and muffins for the morning rush.

"He mixed everything, poured the batter into the pans, cut the cookies, and kept track of the time. After Mom got them out of the oven, T.J. boxed everything and made each sale. Can you believe that? He was only five, but he saw everything done hundreds of times, heck thousands of times. Though T.J. worked hard, I told Mom the idea was silly, and we couldn't find a way to legally pay him. That's when she secretly opened a trust and put his wages in it from her salary. Years later I agreed to a trust and that's when Mom told me what she did."

"I didn't know that. I mean, I know most of it, but I assumed it all happened later."

"T.J. has poured as much blood, sweat, and tears

into Christmas Town as much as Mom and Dad. He's cooked, cleaned, mowed, painted, hammered, and swept every part of the property. This place means everything to him, so when he's willing to give it up, we have a problem. A problem bigger than The Ridge."

"I get that. I do, but I'm just afraid."

"Of what?"

"Of taking things down. If we remove mini-golf, then it's like we're removing a part of Mom and Dad." Jonathan leaned back in his chair and grinned like a plotting Grinch. "What's with the look?"

"I have an idea."

30

Where Did We Leave Off?

T.J. got out of his truck and walked across the road. Sydney stood at her trailer door, grinning as he made his way over. T.J. didn't wave, smile, or talk as he came to the front steps.

"I'm surprised to see you back so soon." Sydney flashed her devilish grin, the one that T.J. missed seeing. "Want to come in?"

"Actually, I was wondering if I could take you out?" Sydney bit her lip and stared at him. The silence caused a bit of panic and his heart started to race. "I—"

"Out? Would this out be like going on a date or would it be a business outing?"

"You know we lost a lot of time to truly get to know one another." Sydney nodded. "And tonight is still far off, so why keep wasting time? Let's pick up where we left off without business."

Sydney took a step down. "To be fair, I'm not sure where we left off."

"Me either. So, let's make it official and call this a first date?"

T.J. knew that was a question, but he felt like he was begging. "I'd like that. Let me get my purse." T.J. felt the weight of the world lift off his shoulders. For the past couple of months, he'd been trying to dodge feelings and find a balance between personal and business life. None of it mattered now. Sydney stepped out, closed the door, and asked, "Where are we going?"

T.J. grinned and answered, "Someplace familiar, but also new."

"I guess that could be a lot of places around here."

"True."

Once in the truck, they were off to Christmas Town, and they came to a stop at T.J.'s cabin. Sydney got out of the truck and looked around as T.J. made his way over.

"This is familiar but it's a bit soon for the unfamiliar don't you think?" Sydney's smirk held devilish intent.

T.J. chuckled and answered, "The unfamiliar is that way." He pointed in the direction of the heart of Christmas Town, and they started their trek down the road they just came in on.

They stopped in front of a sign stating Mrs. Claus' bakery. If the sign wasn't enough to give their location away, the smell of freshly baked cookies, cupcakes, and muffins filling the air was enough of a clue.

"Am I finally going to get to sample the world-renowned Christmas Town cookies?"

"Yes, but we aren't going to just go in and get one."

Sydney shook her head. "How else are we going to get one?"

T.J. didn't answer, instead leading the way inside. There was nothing flashy or decorative. It was simply a large kitchen. Three large islands were located in the center of the room. The far side of the room had a counter and cabinets that ran almost the whole length of the room. Ovens were on the back wall and the wall closest to them had a refrigerator, sinks, and storage for pans.

"Sydney, this is Mary Beth, Jessica, and Jennifer. They are the primary chefs at Christmas Town."

Mary Beth walked over, and after wiping her hands on her apron, she held out her hand. "Nice to finally meet you, Ms. Garcia. We've heard a lot about you." Sydney embraced her hand with her own, and before she could ask, Mary Beth added, "Both good and bad, but none of that matters. I've been here since—" She looked at T.J.

"A few years after grandma opened this building," T.J. finished.

"So just a few years." Mary Beth winked. She held out her arms. "It's not the fanciest of kitchens but it gets the job done."

"Speaking of which, do you mind if I have the kitchen for a bit?" T.J. asked.

Mary Beth turned and looked at the clock. "How long is a bit? We have to get the dessert orders started in about an hour."

"An hour will be plenty of time. I'm just going to bake some cookies is all."

"*You're* going to bake?" Sydney gasped.

"Shouldn't be so shocking since I did cook for you before."

Mary Beth cleared her throat. "We'll be back in an hour."

"Thank you."

Mary Beth and the others took their leave as T.J. took off his coat. He walked over and placed it on the coat rack resting opposite the door. He then picked up a stool that sat beside the coat rack and took it over to one of the islands.

He patted the seat and instructed, "Take a seat."

"You certainly know how to treat a girl." Sydney sauntered over to the stool, swaying her hips all the way. "A front-row seat."

"Not just any seat either. This is my seat."

Sydney gently sat down and asked, "Your seat? Like you're the only one who can sit here?"

T.J. started to go through the cabinets and began grabbing all the ingredients he needed. He walked over to the fridge and did the same. He then placed all the items on the island and explained, "My grandfather built that chair for my grandma. They didn't have a lot when they started. Don't get me wrong, it was as nice of a place then as it is now, but luxury items like stools were reserved for the guests. To keep Grandma from being on her feet while things were cooking, he made her the stool.

"It became my stool when I started working here, which was at like five or six. I don't remember everything, but I do know that much of my upbringing was spent in this kitchen. I sat in one of those restaurant toddler booster chairs until I was big enough to sit on the stool. I must have watched her bake ten, maybe twenty thousand cookies before I started working."

Sydney raised her hand as if she were in school. T.J. nodded and she asked, "When I looked this place up online, the bakery was located beside Santa's workshop. I'm fairly certain I remember it still being there the last time I was here."

"You are correct." T.J. held up a flour-coated finger. "That was the original bakery and is used as a point of sale now. When business started to boom, Grandma needed more room with larger ovens, so they built this place and took the finished product over to the store for sale."

Sydney leaned over to gaze out the window. "That has got to suck during the winter."

"It can, but if the weather is too bad, we will close." T.J. once more raised his flour-coated finger. "Well, we're closed to the public, but the kitchen stays open." T.J. locked eyes with Sydney's blank stare. "What?"

She shrugged her shoulders. "Oh, I don't know. Maybe I'm just waiting to hear why you close but keep a kitchen open for a place that won't have customers."

"Oh." T.J. shook his head. "We have a deal with the diner to sell our baked goods when we're closed. It keeps people from taking unnecessary risks by driving out here."

"Instead, you put yourself at risk by driving into town?" T.J. nodded. "Why do it? I mean I know you're a good guy, but that's a bit much, don't you think? If I can go a day without my morning muffin, bagel, or donut, then I'm sure anyone can."

"There are many who drive an hour out of their way every morning to get their breakfast, morning snack, or just a treat. Some come once a week to load up until their next trip. People take time to help us on a good day, and I want to be there for them on the bad. If stopping by the diner to grab their daily delight will make a cold and snow-filled commute better and safer, then it's worth it."

"So, if selling at the diner would be better for people on a bad day, then why isn't it better for them on a good day?"

"We only make a dollar on each dozen items sold, and we allow the diner to keep the profits for the snow days since they do all the work with serving. If we were to sell at the diner on a daily, then we would have to raise costs to cover the loss of business."

"And part of the reason you sell so much is because the price is so low."

T.J. tapped his nose. "We only raise costs for an increase of ingredients."

"How many snow days do you have a year?"

"One or two during a mild winter and about nine or ten during a harsh winter." T.J. shrugged his shoulders. "Trying to figure out how often you'll be closed?"

Sydney chuckled. "That never hurts, but I was just wondering how often you go into debt on snow days. I'm assuming that several hundred to almost a couple thousand are lost each time you close like that."

"The diner pays for the cost of making everything, and either myself or my uncle will make the cookies and deliver them. We are a green energy business, so it essentially costs nothing to run the ovens, and we sell so many cookies that a new oven is paid for after a year of purchase."

"You sell that much?"

T.J. started laughing. "I know this is going to sound unbeliev-able, but the average non-local visitor leaves here with no less than three dozen baked goods. We average almost two thousand visitors a year. That's almost six grand from people just leaving here, and a new oven costs upwards of ten grand."

"That's impressive, but I'm starting to think I'm not going to get to taste these wonderful cookies."

"We're almost there." T.J. began placing the balls of cookie dough on the cookie sheet.

"Oh, can I have some cookie dough?"

"Absolutely not," T.J. snapped. His eyes widened when he realized his tone. "I'm sorry. I didn't mean it like that."

Sydney squinted and peered into what T.J. assumed was his soul. "There's a story there."

T.J. took a deep breath. He loved the memories of his grandmother but speaking to others about them without getting emotional was difficult. "When anyone would ask my grandma that, they would get a story, and if they were foolish enough to try to grab a piece, they would get a slap to the hand."

"Keep going," Sydney urged.

"She used to say that these cookies are the most ordinary cookies one can make, but the reason they're so good is that they're made with love. But if you take part of it away—" T.J. moved one cookie dough ball to the side. "Even the smallest piece—" He pinched off a piece and moved it to the side. "Then you've stolen what makes them special."

"Do you believe that?"

"Honestly, I do. I know it seems silly but everything we make goes toward taking care of a member of the community, and the community takes care of us. If we take something from the community that helped us, then we don't deserve to be here."

T.J. placed the piece of dough into the ball it came from, holding it up.

"Are those her words or yours?"

"A mix of both and a dash from her grandmother."

"I wish I could have met her. I think we would've gotten along."

"She would've loved you." T.J. took the cookie sheet to the

oven, put it on the top rack, and set the timer. "So, there's something else I have to tell you."

"I'm not so sure I like that tone. Is—" Sydney paused, and a look of fear took hold. Her mouth was wide and her eyes wider. "Is this something that I'm going to like?"

"I don't know how you're going to feel about it, but it affects me more than you." T.J. cleared his throat. "I don't know if my aunt will sign your proposal."

"Oh."

"Yeah, well, it gets worse."

"How so?" Sydney asked.

"I told my aunt and uncle that if they refuse to sign, then they need to buy me out."

"You did *what*?" Sydney shouted. "Why would you do that? This place means everything to you."

T.J. nodded. "It does. There isn't an inch of this property that my foot hasn't touched. I've given everything to this place and it's because of how much I've given that I have to walk away."

"I don't follow."

"I can't watch or be part of its downfall. I've done everything I can to save it but there's nothing more I can do. The terrible truth is that The Ridge is what the community needs. We're declining in population and most of the mom-and-pop stores have closed. The Ridge can pump new life into this entire region in ways Christmas Town never could."

"I'm not sure terrible truth is the appropriate phrase, but I understand what you're saying. For what it's worth, I'm sorry about it all."

"Thanks. I just wish I handled things better with you. I shouldn't have tried to block you but work *with* you."

"Me too." Sydney laughed and waved her hands. "I mean, me working with you as well. Let's face it, I was quick to light the fuse and if I had been more honest, upfront, and open, then we could have saved us both some headaches."

"And money," T.J. added.

"Especially that. I ended up shelling out millions more than what I wanted to because of you."

"At least you got a nice house out of it." T.J. grinned.

"I didn't mind paying for that. That view is incredible." T.J. saw Sydney get a glimmer in her eye and her devilish smile returned.

"You're up to something. I can see it." T.J. waved his hand around her entire face.

"I have an idea, but you need to have an open mind."

T.J. shrugged his shoulders. "Sure. I can—I can try that."

"I don't want this to happen, but if Christmas Town were to close, who do you think would buy it?"

"Honestly, I think it wouldn't be to one person. Aside from someone looking to break into farming or maybe cabin rentals, I don't see too many people being interested. I mean, if competition drove us out, what are the odds that someone could come in and compete?" T.J. shook his head. "I think that if we became hard up for money then Uncle Jon would sell the extra land in lots of whatever he can get or maybe as a whole."

"Extra land?" Sydney asked.

"We own almost a thousand acres about twenty miles down the road."

"What do you do with it? Does it have attractions?"

"No. Grandma bought it just after I was born. Christmas Town was doing well but the economy went south. People were losing jobs left and right, struggling to keep food on the table and lights on. She knew they would have a hard time keeping the heat going once winter hit. The land just so happened to go up for auction, and due to times being rough, she was the only one interested and got one heck of a deal.

"She dipped into the business reserve to hire a few of the hardest hit families to help timber some of the land. It was stored on the farm and the amount of wood was ridiculous. We have pictures somewhere of just mountains of cut wood spread out all over the western side of the property. Winter hit the people harder than the economic downturn. Grandma contacted the local churches and came up with a donation system.

"Families who needed firewood were to call their church, and in turn would be given a batch of Christmas Town cookies. Grandma, Jon, and others who worked the farm would make deliveries and get the batch of cookies as a form of payment." T.J. chuckled. "It was this whole elaborate exchange. The family would bring out the cookies and say something like, 'I hear Santa and his elves have a hankering for cookies,' and each time the cookie box was open for everyone to snack on, no matter how full they were."

"That is—"

"Just one of the many stories that make this place special," T.J. explained.

"It is, and it brings me back to your whole making fun of my face thing. Are you familiar with the rent-to-own concept?" T.J.

nodded. "I cannot say this enough—I don't want this to happen —but if Christmas Town were to go under, what do you think about me buying it and then we do a rent-to-own contract?"

"I don't know." T.J. stopped moving. He looked at Sydney as if he were trying to solve a trigonometry question. "I mean it's super generous and I'd love to say yes, but I'm not sure it'd be right." He could feel his mouth open and close, but nothing was coming out. T.J. raised his arm and used his forearm to wipe his forehead. He cleared his throat and continued, "How would it look if I get bought out and then enter a rent-to-own agreement with the person who caused my family business to do under?"

"That's a good point, and for the record once more, I don't want it to happen. But know it could be an option."

"I appreciate it. I really do. I just hope my aunt wakes up and signs the non-compete." T.J. looked over at the timer. "Are you ready?"

"For?"

T.J. pointed in the direction of the cookies and walked to the oven. He pulled out the cookie sheet and took it to the island where he placed each cookie on the cooling rack. Next, he went to a cabinet and returned with cups, plates, and two forks. T.J. then retrieved the milk from the fridge and filled their cups.

"The best cookie you've ever had." T.J. slid a cookie on the plate and pushed it toward Sydney. "I'm fine with them cold, but to me, they are best right out of the oven."

Sydney picked up her fork, cut off a piece, lightly blew on it, and then took a bite. As she chewed, T.J. saw her eyes light up and a smile spread across her face. It was a similar smile to those of his nieces and nephews on Christmas morning as they rushed into the living room to see their gifts.

T.J. handed her a cup of milk and asked, "What do you think?"

Sydney took a sip and declared, "You're a liar." She waved her hand over the cookie. "This isn't an ordinary cookie. There's something more than basic ingredients. What's the secret?"

"You saw everything I put into it—there's nothing special."

"Fine." Sydney cut off another piece. "Then I'm going to believe that your secret is love." She ate another piece. "But I have one last question."

"Go on."

"Are you sure you can walk away from here?"

31

Time's Up

Sydney escorted Beth and Jonathan to the kitchen table where T.J. and Juan were already seated.

"Beth, Jonathan, it's good to see you both." Juan extended his hand.

Jonathan embraced the handshake. "You as well."

Beth shook his hand too and said, "Thanks for meeting with us."

"Of course. I've gotten to see much of this town while I waited, and I see why you're so protective of it. It reminds me of the village I grew up in. But you're not here to listen to tails of my childhood."

"There will be time for that, but we do have an answer," Jonathan informed. He looked at T.J., then at Beth, and back to Juan. "We can't accept unless you add one thing."

"One thing?" Juan asked. He was as perplexed as T.J., but

his voice beamed with excitement. "I'm not sure I've ever had a business deal when only one thing was requested. Please, tell me."

"We want all current community members to get free lifetime access to all areas of the amusement park and a quick line pass. Oh, and a soft opening for the community only. So, like two or three things."

"That's all?" Sydney asked. "You don't want more money or to give up other attractions instead of what's on the table?"

"Your offer is already more than generous, and though it will be difficult to see what we have gone, it will be the best thing for Christmas Town in the end," Jonathan explained.

"Truth be told, the one thing we can't give up is T.J." Beth looked at Jonathan who was bobbing his head at her. "And I'm sorry for the way I've acted. I was worried and the worst in me came out."

"Water under the bridge," Juan comforted.

Beth cleared her throat and announced, "There's just one more thing I'd like to make sure of before we put pen to paper." Juan waved her on. "I want to make sure that before any expansion on The Ridge is done we are consulted."

Sydney wasted no time replying. "With my father's approval, I'm going to speak for him and the company." Juan nodded. "We'll honor the non-compete, but we'll need to put a procedure in place so that everyone is aware of plans to build by The Ridge and Christmas Town. It's important to remember that this contract goes for both of us. Also, keep in mind that this is a formality. We will have the same paperwork and all minor details, like the procedure, finalized by the lawyers before the new year. We'll meet again, and once everyone is good, then we will sign the final contract, the check will be printed, and we'll toast to a long and prosperous future together."

Jonathan pushed over the contract to T.J. "We've both signed. It's your turn."

T.J. grabbed the contract and looked at Beth. "I know this has been tough for you, and I know it's not easy, but it is appreciated."

"Honestly, I'm not sure if you were bluffing or not, but we couldn't risk it. You're the future of Christmas Town."

T.J. grabbed a pen from the table, turned to the last page, and signed. Once the pen lifted from the paper, T.J. closed the contract. He took a deep breath and passed it over to Sydney. She took the contract, turned to the last page, and added her signature.

"We have a little tradition at the company when we sign a contract, and this is no different. So, how about a steak dinner?" Sydney asked.

"I've never been one to turn down a steak," Jonathan proclaimed.

32

Small-Town Dating

T.J. entered the flower shop and walked to the counter. He leaned over to see if Mrs. Jones was crouching behind, but she wasn't there. He looked around and with no one to be found he called out, "Mrs. Jones."

There was a brief silence and a sudden loud cry, "Coming!" It took a moment, but the storeroom door opened fully and a dirt-covered Mrs. Jones appeared. "Sorry for the wait, T.J. These old bones don't move as quickly as they used to."

"You're as spry as ever." T.J. waved his hand around the dirt covering her. "I hope I didn't cause that by startling you."

She looked down to see the black patches on her apron. "Indirectly, but this comes with the territory."

T.J. tilted his head and squinted. "What do you mean indirectly?"

"Well, as you know I don't carry Night Riders and thanks to your standing weekly order, I have to carry them."

"Have to?" T.J. asked.

Mrs. Jones held up her hands. "Poor choice of words. You know I don't mind and I certainly don't mind seeing those beauties arrive, but I knocked one over and—" she pointed to the apron. "here we are."

"Have you thought about growing them yet?"

Mrs. Jones leaned in and winked. "Things going well for the most powerful couple in Fenton?"

"I wouldn't go that far." T.J. blushed. "But, things are going well."

"So well that you've used the L-word?"

T.J. cleared his throat and tugged at his collar. "I believe you owe me some flowers."

Mrs. Jones swatted at the counter. "Shoot, I thought I had you going. I'll be right back." A few moments later she came back holding a bouquet of Night Riders sounded by white lilies. "Here you go."

"Gorgeous as always." T.J. pulled out his card and said, "Round up please."

T.J. walked out and made his way toward his car. As he approached, T.J. noticed a new truck parked beside his. The window rolled down and the voice behind the tinted glass greeted, "You know, you've started something that you can't stop now."

T.J. walked up to the window. "The funny thing is she thinks they're for her."

"Is that so?"

"Indeed." T.J. held up the flowers. "She told me these were favorites, but what she didn't know is that they are also mine."

"Never pictured you for a flower man."

"Is that right? I mean, a tree isn't that different than a flower."

"That's true, but why are these your favorite?"

"When I was a kid I learned about the yin and yang concept and in a way, I felt like it was the perfect example of my life. I had to have everything in balance in my life, even flowers." T.J. drew a circle around both rings of flowers with his fingers. "Six white and six black. Well, violet black but close enough."

Sydney poked her head out of the window. "You're so full of it. Can I have my flowers now?" T.J. handed them over. "Thank you. Now, get in."

T.J. walked over to the passenger side and got in. "I like the truck better than the sedan."

"Thanks. It's still an EV, but much better suited for the area."

"I agree and may I ask where we are going. Or am I being kidnapped?"

"It would technically only be kidnapping if I asked for a ransom." Sydney turned to T.J. and grinned. "I'm rich as sin so this would be abduction."

"Do I want to know why you know that distinction?"

Sydney tapped T.J. on the leg. "Relax. You listen to enough true crime podcasts then you're going to pick up a thing or two."

"Just for the record, I've already told everyone that if I go missing you're the reason behind it."

Sydney started laughing and when it subsided she said, "I've got a surprise for you."

T.J. could feel the smile sweep across his face. "It's not often that I get something, so I'm excited."

"Speaking of being excited. I was asked three times today about our wedding date."

T.J. chuckled. "Welcome to small-town dating."

"Yeah, but it's only been like—" With the sudden stop, T.J. looked at Sydney. He could tell the gears were turning. She squeaked, "Three months. Give or take a week or three."

"You don't know how long it's been, do you?"

Sydney coughed, bent toward the steering wheel, and gazed out the windshield. "I think we might be getting a storm today."

"Oh no, missy. You're not getting off the hook for this."

"In my defense. It's been a crazy year and we never fully decided on when we started dating. If we go back to the first date then it's more than three months, but if we're counting the second first date then it's been three." Sydney looked at T.J., who was pointing up. "Four months. It's been four months."

"I'm just messing with you. It's only been three." Sydney promptly smacked T.J.

"Don't do that!"

"Sorry couldn't help it." Still laughing, T.J. said, "Welcome to small-town dating. There can be some expectations of getting married quickly, but the truth is they just want to see how things are going between us. Asking, 'When's the wedding?' is their way of getting the dirt while also dropping a seed of manipulation."

"Seed of manipulation?"

T.J. cleared his throat. "Well, they ask you about it. You say that things are great but it's too soon for wedding plans. Once they leave, you start thinking about it and then you mention to your partner—" T.J. pointed to himself. "they asked about marriage. It then gets us talking about it and before you know we will start seriously talking about our plans."

"Oh my god!"

T.J. went from being relaxed to sitting as vertically as one could get. "What?" he started scanning the area. "What's wrong?"

"That's exactly what they've done." Relaxing, T.J. started to laugh. "Those deceitful old ladies played me!"

T.J. did his best to stop laughing and they continued on their journey in silence. They drove three miles past The Ridge's construction site and turned onto a dirt road. T.J. looked out Sydney's window so he could see the progress being made. He tried not to make it obvious, but the way he was leaning forward to see past Sydney and back to see out the rear window made it clear.

"You know I can take you around the site any time you want," Sydney informed.

"I'll take you up on it soon, but I have to ask. If we're not going to the site, then where are we going?"

"Not far now." Ten minutes passed and Sydney turned left onto another dirt road. "Know where we are now?"

"To be fair, I've always known where we are." Sydney chuckled and shook her head. "What?"

"Nothing. It's just that even surprising you isn't really surprising you."

"My grandmother used to say the same thing."

The truck came to a clearing and stopped almost in the middle. Sydney got out and T.J. followed her to the front of the truck.

"So, full disclosure." T.J. waved her on. "I'm not exactly sure if we're in the right spot, but this is just a symbolic gesture."

"I'm listening."

"The last house on company property is going to be reserved for me and you." Sydney pointed to the farm in the distance. "I think that is Mrs. Jefferson's property and the access road connects to here."

"It is and it does, but what do you mean reserved for us? Do you mean so we can—"

Sydney slapped his arm. "Get your head out of the gutter. No, this house is going to be a sanctuary for us both. Whenever the stress of work gets to us then we call or text *Sanctuary* and we'll both meet here as quickly as possible, but there will be one rule."

"I'm all ears."

"There will be no business discussed. Not even what the problem is. We'll come here and nothing outside the house exists until we leave." T.J. turned to Sydney and stared intently into her eyes. "You hate the idea don't you?"

The stern look faded as he laughed. "No, I love it. I just couldn't pass on the chance to mess with you." T.J. walked away from the truck with his arms in the air so he could feel the breeze. He twirled around until he was face to face with Sydney. "Thank you."

She wrapped her arms around him and whispered, "You're welcome."

33

❦

Nine Months Later

T.J. poked his head through the doorway and yelled, "Marty!"

"Back here!"

T.J. continued in the restaurant and walked back to the kitchen. He found Marty working away and the warming ovens were filled with pizzas.

"You missed Mr. White's funeral," T.J. informed.

Marty stopped topping the pizza and glared at T.J. Almost growling, he asked, "Do you know why I missed it?"

T.J. shrugged and held up his arms. "I'm going to take a shot here. You were working."

"Yes, I've been working. Do you know why I've been working?" T.J. shook his head. "Because that old mule put in his will that I'm to make one pizza for every year he was alive to be served at the celebration of life service."

T.J. looked at the warming ovens and the pizzas on the

prep table. "That's starting in like ten minutes and you don't have enough."

"Jeremy is currently delivering twenty. There's twenty more warming and even less being made while I stand here and talk to you." Marty looked at T.J. His eyes were bloodshot and water-filled. "Might as well lend a hand while you're here."

T.J. removed his coat and put on an apron. He walked to the mixer, pulled out some dough, and walked to the prep counter. As he started to knead the dough, T.J. kept looking at Marty. He was fighting with his emotions as he sniffed and mumbled while wiping his face. His fist pounded into the dough like he was sending a jab into a punching bag.

Throughout the years, he saw Marty go through the passing of his wife, loss of friends, and he even fought off cancer. While going through some of the worst tragedies a person could go through, Marty never showed sorrow. He was the rock for everyone and used humor like no one else could to turn tears of sadness into tears of joy. Marty reminded everyone of the good regardless of his struggle. But now, Marty wasn't the strong one.

T.J. stopped prepping, stepped over to Marty, turned him around, and pulled him into a hug. Marty finally let out all the years of pain.

"Why didn't he want me there? Why don't I get the chance to say goodbye?" The question was muffled by the quiver in his voice.

Marty pulled away and walked out of the kitchen. T.J. turned off the ovens and followed. Marty poured two cups of soda, his hand shaking as he held one out for T.J.

"I think you know why," T.J. answered.

"No, I don't. I deserve to say— he was like a brother to me. He—"

"He did what was best for you," T.J. interrupted. "Mr. White knew how difficult it would be for you to be there, and he spared you that pain."

"He didn't spare me from anything. He traded one pain for another."

Marty could no longer look T.J. in the eye. His head hung low, and his hands moved frantically across his face to wipe the tears away.

"You know what I never understood?" T.J. asked. Marty just shrugged. "Why is it that people say they never got to say good-bye at the funeral? Why do we have to say goodbye at all? We spend years with some and decades with others building this house of memories. Rooms filled with joy, rooms crowded by sorrow, and others scattered with a bit of both. When someone says they're saying a final goodbye, it's like barricading a house you'll never go into again. As long as we remember them, as long as we speak of them, then they're never gone."

"You have a point."

"Of course, I do. Everything I say has meaning." Marty laughed and pointed at T.J. "In the grand scheme of life, Grandma hasn't been gone long but everywhere I go around town there's something that jogs a memory. Like—" T.J. turned and walked to the end of the counter where the kitchen opens to the dining area. He looked and pointed. "There." T.J. walked over to the chair. "Right here. When I was six. Do you remember?"

Marty looked over and a smile began to creep along his

face. It grew as fast as a sloth climbing a tree, but he knew what T.J. was talking about.

"We were swamped, and Sara came to the back to help while you waited on your order." Marty walked over to T.J. and turned back to the kitchen. "We finally got to your pizza and while Sara was bringing it out, she tripped." Marty walked to the spot. "And the pizza flew off the pan and onto your head."

"Do you remember what happened next?" T.J. asked.

"You thought it was the funniest thing in the world and started eating the toppings and cheese in your hair."

"And off the table." T.J. pointed at Marty. "But not the floor." Their laughter now melded together in harmony.

Marty took a seat at the table. "I know this is going to be hard to believe but I wasn't always this muscular. When I started high school, I was a hundred pounds soaking wet...with rocks in my pockets. School was different for us back then, but the kids were the same. The moment I stepped into the building I became a target.

"This baseball star who went by the nickname Slugger was drawn to me like a moth to a flame. If there was a way to torment someone, then Slugger did it to me. It went on for weeks until one day Hue stepped in—and I mean stepped in. Age whittled him down but back then he was a grizzly bear of a teenager. Hue just stood there, towering over Slugger. It was a stare-down to end all stare-downs. With each second the tension built but no one moved or even talked. I like to think that Slugger was imagining the whooping that would ensue if there was a fight. Ultimately, Slugger backed down and walked away. From that day on, Hue and I were the best of friends."

"It worked, didn't it?" T.J. asked.

"It did." Marty nodded. "It was like it happened yesterday."

"You know, I promised Mr. White that I'd turn his house into a museum to memorialize his and his family's history. These are memories that pictures can't convey. Memories that tell the good about someone. So, when you're ready, I'd like you to write down these good times with Mr. White. I'll put them in a booklet and place them around the house so people will know how great he was."

"I'd be happy to."

"Good. Now, let's get back to cooking. I'm not going to be haunted by a grizzly ghost because you decided to pout instead of fulfilling someone's wishes."

"Oh, T.J., you only have to worry about *me* haunting you."

34

Christmas

T.J. cracked open the office door and asked, "Are you ready?"

"Come on in, and almost," Sydney answered.

T.J. walked in and saw Sydney's body being hugged by a black dress; it outlined every curve and had a thigh-high slit running up her left leg.

"You look amazing."

Sydney looked up from the folder to see T.J. in a black tuxedo. "And you—" T.J. did a model-like turn. "I've never seen you this dressed up. We need to find more formal events to attend."

"You like?" T.J. asked.

"*Love*. You look great." Sydney placed the folder on the table and walked to T.J. "I'll be glad when we're up and running."

Sydney wrapped her arms around T.J. and kissed him. When she pulled back, he asked, "Everything okay?"

"Yeah, just a small delay with some materials. It'll put us about three weeks behind schedule."

"That's not too bad," T.J. comforted.

"True. I mean, we'll be finished with construction midway through next winter and have about three months before a spring opening, so it doesn't hurt too bad." Sydney walked over to her office window and looked at the growing resort. "Hard to believe that it's already been over a year."

"Over a year and yet, this will be your first Christmas."

Sydney turned to T.J. "I was here last Christmas."

T.J. shook his head back and forth. "Technically, you're right. You were here during the Christmas season, but you flew out before Christmas day, so this will be your first Christmas here."

"That's true." Sydney grabbed T.J.'s hand and began pulling him to the exit. "It also means that you better make this one worth remembering."

T.J. did his best not to smile while being dragged. "It seems like you're more excited about this than I am."

"Of course, I am. I'm not the one speaking, so tonight is a big win for me but an even greater one for you and your family." T.J. took a deep breath and looked up. Sydney stopped and asked, "Are *you* okay?"

T.J. exhaled and locked eyes with Sydney. "Not at all."

"You want to talk about it?"

T.J. shrugged his shoulders. "I'm not prepared for this. I planned and gathered everything but wasn't involved with the final production. I don't know what's inside and I'm worried."

"About what?"

"Grandma."

"Are you worried that she'd be upset with the deal we made?"

"No. I'm certain she would have done the same. No, I'm worried about myself. I know she's going to be all over, and I'm worried about how I'm going to react."

"Oh, well." Sydney took T.J.'s hands and cupped them with hers. "How you react will be how you react. No one is going to think any less of you if you get emotional. Tonight is going to be emotional for most, if not everyone, there."

T.J. took another deep breath. "You're right."

"Of course, I am." Sydney grinned.

The car ride was silent, and as they pulled into Christmas Town there wasn't an empty parking spot. He continued up the road to his cabin and saw hundreds of candles lighting up the night.

"Great turnout," Sydney noted.

"They've always been there for us," T.J. whispered, holding back his feelings.

After parking, T.J. and Sydney took a stroll to the stage. She held his hand tightly and the two remained silent. As he walked up to the podium the candles had grown in numbers. T.J. looked out and gazed upon what seemed like the entire county.

"I want to start by thanking everyone for coming tonight. I speak for all of my family." T.J. turned to look at Beth and Jon, and then he looked to the sky. "Those here and those who've passed, we're blessed to have had your support and friendship for all these years. I say friendship, but the word isn't quite fitting because you've become family. For decades you've made Grandma's dream not just a reality but a thriving business.

A business with a mission not to just provide a place to escape from daily struggles, but one that gives back to the community.

"It is the continuation of this partnership that brings us here tonight. When I read the headline about the resort coming I, like many of you, panicked. Though some of my family thought I wasn't concerned, I can assure them and everyone here that I was like—" T.J. stopped and snickered. "Grandma could always tell what I was feeling. She used to say, 'Stop being a duck.'" Many in the crowd, familiar with her phrases, chuckled. "She knew that though I looked okay on the outside, everything on the inside was going a mile a minute, much like a duck swimming. Calm above the water and frantically panicking below the surface.

"The truth is that when faced with the competition, we were over-extended. I also made some stupid choices that would've ruined me in less than a decade. However, I came to realize that I was being selfish. Grandma loved this town because of the people in it, and the people are hurting. If closing the doors to Christmas Town would result in helping the community, then she would've done it in a heartbeat. She would want people to have jobs with benefits and not to worry about where their next meal would come from. By the time I realized this, Ms. Garcia offered a partnership."

"In more ways than one!" Steven shouted inappropriately.

After the laughing subsided, T.J. informed, "That's my best friend, everyone." T.J. looked at Sydney who was grinning, not showing the slightest hint of anger. "We were offered a non-compete and the decision to work together instead of against was made. As you know we've removed several attractions while adding a couple of buildings. We then reached out to ask for pictures and videos of the times spent here. Within a day we had hundreds of both to sort through. After a month, we had hundreds of thousands, and we're still getting material. Only a few of you knew why, and you're here tonight under somewhat false pretenses. You're here to see a new attraction.

"I'm sure many thought there would be some neat ride or something cool that would compete with The Ridge. However, I'm going to disappoint some, but not for long. Though I don't know what it looks like inside, I know you're going to love it because a part of us can be found inside. The attraction behind me is a tribute to Christmas Town. It's a memorial to friends and family who are no longer with us. It's a bridge that connects the past behind us to what lies ahead."

T.J. pressed the first button on the remote resting on the podium. The night sky became illuminated as the lights all over Christmas Town glowed. The large black curtain behind T.J. came into full view, and though it was large, it wasn't big enough to hide the entire structure behind it. Without delay, T.J. pressed the second button on the remote and the curtain bolted to the ground, revealing the largest building on the property.

It had the rustic cabin look like the others on the property, but there was a second floor. A covered porch hosted a sign on top that mirrored the one at the entrance, but it had the title Museum added under Christmas Town. Lights wrapped around the gutters and along the edges of the building and the soft white glow allowed everyone to soak in the magnitude of the structure. The audience erupted in cheers, applause, whistles, and shouts.

T.J. took a step back from the podium and covered his mouth as he looked at the crowd, he did everything he could to hold back how he felt. No one was disappointed that they were seeing a museum and not some theme ride. He knew that they would have been supported, but seeing is believing. Before T.J. could say anything else, Sydney popped up by his side and took the microphone.

"Greetings, everyone. The doors will open in just a few minutes, and we are going to ask everyone to form a line to the left of the building." Sydney pointed to the far end of the museum. "There will be a bin for you to place your candles but there's just one more thing I must ask of you. We've prepared a bit of a surprise for T.J."

T.J. covered the microphone and asked, "What surprise?"

"It wouldn't be a surprise if we told you about it." Sydney smacked his hand away and announced, "We need about ten more minutes before we let everyone in."

"What are you up to?"

Sydney grabbed T.J.'s arm and once more led him away. "You'll see." They arrived at the entrance doors where she ordered, "Close your eyes."

T.J. did, and she led him inside. With each step, his heart beat faster and faster. His mind raced with ideas of what could be awaiting him, and the anticipation took him back to his childhood. It brought back the memories of his grandmother telling him to close his eyes and open his mouth wide as she used him as a taste tester for new desserts. T.J. couldn't help smiling and giggling at the thoughts.

"I'm going to help you turn around and you must look at me and only me. Do you understand?" Sydney sternly asked.

"Yes, but won't I be facing the exit?" T.J. asked.

"Do you understand?" Sydney asked again.

"Yes," T.J. answered. Sydney spun him around and T.J. opened his eyes. He looked at Sydney who was holding a letter. "What's this?"

"Your grandmother wrote you a letter before she passed." Sydney handed it to T.J. and he carefully began to open it.

He unfolded the pages and read, "My dearest T.J."

But it wasn't just his eyes that read the words; a voice behind him called out. It wasn't just any voice... it was hers. The voice behind him was unmistakable—it was his grandmother's. Without hesitation, T.J. spun around to come face-to-face with her. Sara was being projected on a digital display and dressed as Mrs. Claus.

"I knew at some point that things would get tough for Christmas Town, and I knew there would be one person who would hold it together. I love your aunt and uncle with all my heart, but they don't think as you do. Tough decisions will have to be made to ensure the magic goes on, and I'm certain you are the reason it continues.

"As I write this, I'm torn at what to say. There are so many things I wish I could've changed in my life and the way you grew up is one of them. But if I changed that, then I wouldn't have gotten to raise you. The countless hours that we spent together filled my days with nothing but joy. Even now, knowing the end is near, the memories of you sneaking a cookie, marking the putt-putt course—" Sara bent over and whispered, "I always knew you cheated." She winked and stood tall once more. "Or singing along with the radio as we baked away does my heart good.

"Your life here is the very reason Christmas Town exists. From day one this has been a place of new beginnings and second chances. You got that here, and because of you, Christmas Town will get another chance to carry on. I couldn't be prouder of you. You're my grandson on paper but in my heart, you're my son." She raised her hand and T.J. stepped forward. He placed his hand over hers. "I love you."

"Love you too."

T.J. removed his hand from the screen and brushed away the tears of both sorrow and joy. He held the letter tight, turned around, and without saying a word, T.J. rushed out of the museum.

35

Aftermath

"What? I mean—What happened? Should I—" Sydney was baffled. "I thought he'd like it."

Jonathan walked over and put his arm around Sydney. "That wasn't about you."

"Then what was it?"

"You gave him the best gift that anyone could ever give. You gave him the chance to see Mom one more time. He's upset but in the best of ways." Jonathan turned Sydney to the door. "When you see him, just wait until he's ready to talk."

Sydney opened the door and peered. When she didn't see T.J., she closed the door and asked, "Where did he go?"

"If I were a betting man, I'd put all I have on Santa's workshop." Jonathan pointed down the hill. "Bring him back when he's ready."

Sydney walked down the hill, and though Jonathan said

not to worry, she couldn't help it. There's more than one digital display of Sara throughout the museum and each one could be as triggering as the one before it.

Sydney opened the doors to Santa's workshop slowly and stuck her head in to see if T.J. was there. Sure enough, he was sitting on the floor, back to the door, and looking up at Santa's chair. She continued to be as quiet as possible as she entered and walked to T.J.'s side.

He must have sensed her presence because he said, "I'm sorry for running out like that."

"No, I'm sorry," Sydney said, carefully sitting beside him.

"There's nothing to be sorry for," T.J. insisted.

"But it's all my fault. The digital displays were my idea. I had my dad's studio create all of it."

"They're perfect, and I do mean perfect. I swear it was like she was there. It looked, moved, and sounded just like her." T.J. cleared his throat. "I never got to tell her how much she meant to me. Everyone else was here, but I was—"

"Exactly where she wanted you to be, where you needed to be." Sydney placed her hand on T.J.'s leg. "She spared you the greatest of heartaches while giving herself a piece of comfort."

"I—" His voice cracked. He coughed and cleared his throat once more. "I miss her."

Sydney couldn't help imagining the crack in his voice matching what was left in his heart. The wound left behind from missing Sara's funeral is as fresh tonight as it was then. This pain caused T.J. to show his first true sign of emotion around her. Despite a couple of moments of annoyance, T.J. had always been calm and collected. She knew that the only thing she could do was listen.

"I know you do."

T.J. continued to look at the chair, and after a deep breath he asked, "Is that the only display?"

"No, there are several more."

T.J. nodded. "I don't know if I can go back tonight."

"You don't have to. We can stay here or go back to the cabin. Whatever you want is fine with me."

"I had this whole thing planned tonight and I ruined it."

"Nothing is ruined. If anything, this is the perfect way to spend the night."

T.J. huffed. "Sitting on the floor watching me hold back tears isn't perfect."

Sydney stood up and tugged at T.J. to do the same. He did, and finally, they locked eyes.

"We're here so that we can celebrate the history of Christmas Town, right?" T.J. nodded. "What better place to be than where it all began." Sydney twirled around. "This is where your grandparents started it all. The memories are up there, but the history is here."

"It is," T.J. agreed. "I'm hoping it's where it will continue."

"Of course, it will." Sydney finished twirling, and upon looking at T.J., she noticed him motioning his eyes to Santa's chair. "What's wrong?"

"Go see," he said.

Sydney walked over to the throne-like chair and noticed a red box resting on the cushion. Her pace slowed as she realized what it potentially could be, but her heart began to race. She climbed up the two steps, walked over to the chair, and grabbed the box.

T.J. was now on the other side of the chair, and with her mouth wide open, she just looked at him.

"When I had planned this, I wasn't picturing myself with bloodshot eyes and being a blubbering mess." T.J. gently took the box from her and opened it. "We're in the place that holds my past, but I'm with the person I want to share my future." T.J. removed the ring from the box and took Sydney's hand. Gently, he placed the ring on her finger. "As long as she'll have me."

With the ring secured on her finger, Sydney jumped and wrapped her arms around T.J. She whispered in his eye, "Of course, I will."

T.J. held tight, lifted her off the ground, and spun her around.

From across the room a loud, "Um-hum" called out. T.J. stopped abruptly and the pair turned to the owner of the voice. Sydney didn't recognize the person, but T.J.'s glare and clutched jaw signaled he knew them.

The woman took a step forward and announced, "I guess this is my future daughter-in-law."

Author's Note Part II

The journey from idea to print is never easy and is filled with every emotion that one can experience. A step that is critical and an acknowledgment that can go unrecognized is with editing and one's editor.

I owe my editor, Ryan Jones, my deepest thanks for taking me on as a client. Ryan has edited the majority of my books and because of the work she does I often feel like I'm one of the few authors who enjoys editing. There will never be enough words to properly express how grateful I am.

Other Works by D.W. Saur

Dark Days

It has been centuries since The Great War and the four sects of Sori have come to live in relative peace and harmony. Sori's Caomhnóir judges the occasional crimes in Bala's markets and the severity of punishments deter the majority from temptation. Besides the crimes committed in Cala's boundaries, the sects of Sori saw an era of prosperity.

Though the sects prospered, this euphoric state was not destined to last forever. A dark, almost ghost-like, figure arrives in

Sori and begins to upset the balance the land has come to enjoy. The figure plots and manipulates members of the Galenvarg and Veirlintu sects into rebellion. Upon the arrival of the figure, the Goddess Nantosuelta selects a Leigheasan named Maya as her chosen one to eliminate the threat and prevent another Great War.

To many Leigheasan, Maya was not capable of being a chosen one. She had not completed their rite of passage, was powerless, and isolated herself from those her age. With Nantosuelta's blessing, Maya begins her quest to find her powers, prevent war, and establish herself as a leader among the Leigheasan.

Accolades for Dark Days

2022 Book Excellence Awards: Finalist in Young Adult Fiction

2021 Readers' Favorite Book Awards: Honorable Mention in the Young Adult category for Action

2021 American Fiction Awards: Finalist in the Epic/High category

2021 Feathered Quill Book Awards: Finalist in the category of Science Fiction/Fantasy

2021 Feathered Quill Book Awards: Finalist in the category of Teens (13-18)

2020 Royal Dragonfly Book Award: Dark Days won a Royal DragonFly award in the category of Young Adult Fiction

2020 Royal Dragonfly Book Award: Dark Days won a Royal DragonFly award in the category of Science Fiction/Fantasy

5 Star Reader's Favorite Book Seal

4 Star Literary Titan Book Seal

Just Friends

The Fantastic Four leaped out of the pages of the comics and straight into suburbia. Justin, Jill, Sam, and Amanda were born in the same year, lived on the same street, and were insepa-rable during their early childhood. Their bond became tested in middle school when Amanda started to drift from the group. By the time they entered high school, Amanda was rarely seen with her childhood friends.

Throughout high school, Sam was officially placed in Amanda's friend zone and only spoke to him when she needed a shoulder to cry on. No matter how badly he was treated Sam clung to the hope of a relationship but that all changed after being stood up as her date for senior prom. Sam was finally tired of just being Amanda's friend so he severed ties and moved on to college.

There he meets Jennifer and the two begin making the type of memories Sam once wished he could have shared with Amanda. During Sam's freshman year, Amanda kept her distance and they went over a year without communication of any kind. No DMs, no texts, and no calls were made by either of them. This all ends when Amanda comes knocking on Sam's dorm expecting to have his comforting ear once more. However, Amanda discovers Sam has more than just a girlfriend. Sam has been holding on to a secret that will forever change their friendship.

Metal Like Me

As a child, Vinny was unaware of his and his family's difference but, as he got older, Vinny noticed that he was, in fact, not like other children. Because he was a metalhead, Vinny had a hard time making friends in elementary school. This changed as he entered middle school, where Vinny finally found friends who were metal like him. The group did not have an easy time as they were bullied or picked on for much of their first year. Tired of being viewed as different, Vinny came up with a plan to show their classmates that he and his friends weren't that different.

Join Vinny as he shares his story of bullying, difference, coping, and perseverance.

Accolades for Metal Like Me

2020 Purple Dragonfly: Honorable Mention
2020 Story Monsters Approved: School Life
5 Star Reader's Favorite Book Seal
5 Star Literary Titan Book Seal

Scream With Me: Volume I

Does unconditional love truly exist or is love a matter of convenience? Are ghosts real or is our mind playing tricks on us? What if urban legends are not just stories aimed to scare, but frightfully true stories? Scream With Me explores these questions in three chilling parts.

In Unconditional Love, Emma and her daughters are set to begin a new life when it quickly becomes as upside down as the one they had left behind. A new home brings new terrors and reveals love may or may not be unconditional, but it does come with a price.

Jackson's family paid a small fee for a ghost walk in the heart of colonial America. Though many hoped to see a ghost, Jackson just wanted the tour over. His skepticism faded as the group came to the Peyton Randolph House. Something about it made Jackson's skin crawl and he knew that though the building was empty, he was being watched. He began to believe that when he entered he was going to discover the secrets that lay within the walls of The Peyton Randolph House.

Hundreds of miles north is the home to one of the most infamous legends, The Jersey Devil. Many heard the terrifying tale of The Devil as a child, but most thought it was just that, a story. However, Jay refused to dismiss The Devil as make-believe. He insisted that the legend was not just true but was the missing piece of a puzzle that connected hundreds of crimes. With 2023 being the year of The Devil, Jay and his friends will get their chance to catch The Devil or become its victim.

The Last Christmas

Sara's marriage was on the rocks for years. After a long shift, she arrived home to a note saying, "Locks have been changed. Your stuff is on the porch."

Sara grabbed her bags, got back in the car, and headed aimlessly up the highway. For Sale signs act like a homing beacon and lead Sara to a rundown Christmas tree farm. A vision of a farm that brought Santa's village to reality ensued. The owner of the land agrees to sell a portion of the farm for Sara's promise to revive it to its former glory.

With the Herculean task of running and renovating, help unexpectedly comes when a former childhood visitor of the farm named Jack arrives. The duo is committed to bringing a North Pole experience to all but amidst a budding relationship in turbulent times.

The Untold: Stories from World War II

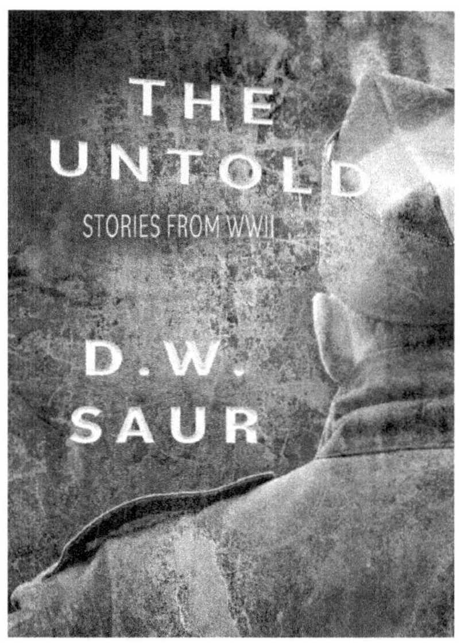

What if the villain isn't who you think he was? What if you are called to risk it all by going behind enemy lines? What if your skills require you to take another's life? The Untold: Stories from World War II is a historical fiction novella divided into three stories that address these questions with a series of twists.

In A Crime Against Humanity, a courtroom full of press and attendees glare at the man accused of murdering thousands of Jews at the concentration camp known as Schwarzes Wasser. Commandant Karl Müller admits to every horrible deed committed in enough detail that his fate is sealed. However, there's more to Karl's story than just the crimes committed.

When Karl's story ends, veteran Luke Taylor retells his story in Flashbacks. Born into a military family, Luke, along with almost fifty other boys, was groomed to be spies in the mission codenamed Project Loki. It took decades for Luke to realize that infiltrating the Nazi war machine was the easiest part of his mission.

The Untold comes full circle in The Eastern Front when a graduate student unlocks the story between the cryptic pages of Oksana Gribanov's diary. The diary reveals her time of service as a sharpshooter during the siege in Leningrad and beyond.

What's New and Where to
Follow

Instagram
@d.w.saur
@polarpressbooks

X (Twitter)
@dw_saur
@polarpressbooks

YouTube
@PolarPressPresents

Goodreads
@dwsaur

Website
https://dwsaur.com/
https://polarpressbooks.com/

www.ingramcontent.com/pod-product-compliance
Lightning Source LLC
Chambersburg PA
CBHW060406310726
48976CB00003B/964